MW00618784

NICOLE

A Sweet Romantic Comedy

SARAH MONZON

RADIANTPUBLICATIONS

Manuscript edited by Katie Donovan

❀ Created with Vellum

1

NICOLE

*I*t is a truth universally unacknowledged that not every woman who is single is in want of a husband.

And I really wished my sewing sisters would get that through their thick skulls.

Because of their endless urging, I entered the restaurant at the appointed time to meet one David Brown (age, thirty-five; height, five foot nine; body type, athletic; occupation, electrician—or so his online dating profile said) that day in October. If Molly, Amanda, Jocelyn, and Betsy hadn't bribed me, I wouldn't have been there at all.

I'd been fine on my own the five years since my ex-husband walked out on me and our daughter. I really had no intention of letting another male mansplain to me why they were essential to a woman's happiness. Newsflash—they're not!

No, my presence at that restaurant had nothing to do with romance or "getting out there" or trying to find "Mr. Right" and everything to do with the fifty dollars each of my friends had pledged to donate to a charity of my choosing every time I agreed to meet with some guy from one of the dating apps they'd set up in my name.

Two hundred dollars, I'd reminded myself when I approached that table, David Brown exhibiting refreshing manners as I neared. His eyes lit on my face but then lowered to check out the rest of me. I got it. Outward appearances mattered to most people. Good thing my heart wasn't set on this guy or anything happening between us, otherwise the way his eyes rounded when his gaze reached my hips would have wounded me.

I'd warned him and every other guy on that archaic yet high tech matchmaker app: body type, curvaceous. Pretty sure Amanda chose that adjective, but the word fit. I have curves. At 174 pounds, maybe some dangerous ones. But the headshot Jocelyn insisted on didn't show the guys trolling and swiping left and right the full picture. My body was like a two-lane country road that all of a sudden exploded into a six-lane major city highway—pear shaped. My top half didn't carry the bulk of my weight. Those pounds congregated around my hips and thighs.

Did my thighs rub together when I walked? Yes. Was it ridiculously hard to find a pair of pants that fit my rear without having a huge gap at the small of my back? Yes. But that's the manufacturer's problem, not mine. I refused to feel shamed because my body didn't fit someone's mold.

Two hundred dollars, I reminded myself again when David Brown's bug eyes finally returned to normal size and he gulped, his cheeks stained red.

"Nice to meet you," he said, but his stiff body language conveyed another message. He'd mentally deleted me from his prospective digital matches.

I set my teeth and forced a grin. "You too." The girls wouldn't make their donation to the Nature Conservancy if I let this worm off his hook, so I lowered onto the seat across from him.

A server approached our table and placed glasses of ice water in front of us.

"Welcome to the Loft. I'm Jen and I'll be your server this evening. Can I start y'all off with some wine?"

David looked at me, eyebrow cocked.

My fingers hugged the cold glass of water, and I pulled it closer. "Water's fine for me, thanks."

David turned to Jen the server. Even from his profile I could see the widening of his eyes. The upturn at the side of his lips. His gaze roamed from the top of Jen's artful messy bun to the tips of her non-skid black loafers—the same once over he'd given me, but this time an appreciative gleam entered his gaze.

"The right guy will make you feel like a princess," Molly had said. Well, sure. When you lived in a fairy tale

where you're engaged to a guy who'd literally given you a rainbow unicorn, you could have an outlook like that. My track record consisted of trolls that made me feel like dirt and should live under bridges while eating the three billy goats gruff.

I rolled my eyes but held my tongue. I was on this date under false pretenses anyway. If David Brown wanted to hit on our server, why should I care? Wasn't like I was here for anything other than the money.

I stilled at that thought and let the faint laughter from Jen pass over me. I could feel a Grinch-grin curling the sides of my lips in evil delight. My friends were pimping me out—not really, I knew that—and I wasn't going to let them off the hook. At least, not without a little more cash thrown in for the Nature Conservancy.

What?! Saving the planet gets expensive, and a hairstylist doesn't exactly rake in the money.

My "date" flirted a bit more, and I stared out the window to give them a small measure of privacy.

"Are y'all ready to order then?"

The question pulled me back around. David looked at me and waited. I wasn't really hungry and hadn't looked at the menu to see if they had any vegan options. "I'll have a garden salad." I handed the still-closed menu to Jen.

"And I'll have a hamburger cooked medium." He glanced at me again. "And extra fries for the table."

Let it go, Nicole. Let him squander his money if he

wanted to. But the wasted money wasn't what bothered me. It was the uneaten food. Restaurants threw out hundreds of pounds of perfectly good food a day while people literally starved down the street.

I smiled sweetly. "That's okay. I don't want any fries."

David frowned, and his eyes flicked down. If he'd had x-ray vision, he'd have been looking through the table to my size sixteen jean-clad hips.

His gaze returned to mine. "You might think you don't want fries now, but when mine come out, you'll change your mind." He looked back to our server with a placating smile. "Extra fries," he said as he handed her his menu.

I beamed brighter at Jen, channeling the rising heat from my core into rays of clipped civility. "Just the salad. No fries for me. Thank you."

Her sculpted eyebrows pulled down as she volleyed her gaze between David and me, wondering which of us she should listen to. I held her gaze a second longer, and she must have seen something in my eyes, because she scurried away with a squeak.

"I don't know what the big deal is. It's just French fries. If you don't want them then you don't have to eat them."

I breathed in through my nose and gripped the edge of the table, my knuckles turning white.

"Don't be so dramatic, Nikki." How many times had I heard those words come out of Greg's mouth?

"Don't be so dramatic. It's only a little fever." Sierra had been six months old, barely breathing, and burning up.

"Don't be so dramatic. It's only a joke." One at which no one laughed, only cried or seethed on the inside.

"Don't be so dramatic. I just had to work late." And have an eight-month affair before running off with Chelsea from human resources.

I pushed my hair back from my shoulders and rolled my lips. This was one of those times I needed to pick my battles. David Brown and our hopefully-no-longer-than-half-an-hour acquaintance wasn't worth a spike in blood pressure.

"Your profile says you enjoy rock climbing?" Maybe I could get him to talk about himself, then tune him out until the check came.

He nodded. "Yeah. It's a great workout, you know." His eyes traveled south again, and he leaned a bit to the side.

Really? Was he really trying to catch a glimpse of my lower half under the table?

"You should check it out sometime." He blinked, seeming to reconsider. "Although, I'm not sure they have…" His voice trailed off.

I knew exactly what he'd left dangling. He wasn't sure they'd have a harness that would fit my body type.

I tilted my head and poured innocence into my voice. "Not sure they have what?"

"Well, you know." He waved his hand in the direction of my legs.

"No, I don't know. Educate me."

He looked away and shifted uncomfortably in his seat.

"Okay then, let me educate *you*."

His head whipped back around.

"In the future, if your date doesn't have the fictional body of a Barbie dream girl, don't stare in horror and take surreptitious glances at what you consider *problem areas*." My fingers hooked in air quotes. "Don't flirt with another woman when you're supposed to be out with a lady. And for goodness' sake"—I scooted back from the table—"don't assume that if a woman isn't your ideal weight she's going to steal your French fries!"

A smattering of applause erupted around us, and I realized my voice had risen with each word until I had practically yelled the last part.

David ducked his head. "You know what? I don't think this is going to work."

I wanted to throw one of Betsy's sarcastic retorts— no kidding, Sherlock!—his way, but refrained.

"I'm just going to go." He was halfway to the door before he'd finished speaking.

My nose scrunched. Great. Now I was left with the check and the dead carcass of a murdered cow. Perhaps I could get it boxed up and find someone on my way home who'd benefit from a free meal.

But the worst part was that the Nature Conservancy would be out a two-hundred-dollar donation.

Maybe if I told the girls about the body shaming I'd had to endure, they'd still write the checks.

Movement out of the corner of my eye brought my head up in time to see a man lower himself into the newly vacated seat across from me.

Over-long maple-syrup-colored hair flopped across a stately brow. Ginger eyes dancing with mirth stared back at me, a grin full of secrets pulling at the corners of his cheeks.

Well, ding dong dilly. Wasn't this my luck. Drew Bauer with his cocky smirk that probably left all the female personnel at the hospital swooning but irritated me like a splinter left to fester.

"Quite a show you put on there."

I huffed.

"Although, I'm surprised you gave him so many strikes before kicking him out of the batter's box. You didn't give me quite so much rope to hang myself with." He leaned his forearms on the table, invading my space.

His presence was like kerosene on my temper, stoking the fire within me to four-alarm proportions. I leaned right back, staring into his ginger orbs, rising to the unspoken challenge.

Everything about Drew Bauer annoyed me. He was a dripping-faucet, nails-on-a-chalkboard, litter-tossed-in-the-streets kind of man all rolled up into one carefree, obnoxious package. I'd been accused of caring too much about too many things, and if that were true then Drew was the anti-me. All nonchalant casualness. Complacent disinterest and apathetic indifference.

A small part of me whispered that couldn't be completely true, since he was a doctor, and doctors had to care about their patients. But then I'd remember his comments about how we needed more oil pipelines and less restriction on pollution from big companies, and my stance on him being a horrible human being would solidify.

"You know"—he continued to smirk at me—"I was five seconds away from laying into that guy myself."

"I don't need you to come to my rescue."

"Of course not. You're strong enough to fight your own battles. I'd never mistake you for a damsel in distress."

I narrowed my eyes at him.

"No, I wasn't going to say anything on your behalf."

"Why then?"

A group of people at an adjoining table burst out laughing. Drew paused for their gaiety to quiet.

"For the male gender, naturally. That jerk was making us all look bad."

My turn to bark out laughter. "A little late to redeem my estimation of the males of our species."

His grin hiked. "We aren't all terrible."

I made a show of considering. "You're right. Ben is a sweetheart." Ben was Drew's colleague and best friend and the fiancé of one of my best friends. Molly and Ben were the reason I put up with Drew. They were also the reason I *had* to put up with Drew.

I grabbed my purse and stood. "As lovely as this evening has been, I'm going to go home."

His hand encircled my wrist to stop my departure. "Not so fast."

I glared at his fingers. "Unhand me."

Instead of obeying, he had the audacity to trail his thumb along the tendon of my inner wrist.

I jerked my arm away.

"I don't think you really want to go," he said smoothly.

"You presume to know what I want?" I challenged.

His eyes rose to meet mine, a flash of victory making them shine bright. "You want to earn the two hundred dollars your friends promised."

My lips pressed together.

"I believe the stipulations were dinner consumed, three topics of conversation, and you let him walk you to your car."

I folded my arms across my chest. "As everyone witnessed, David Brown walked out. My agreement with the girls can no longer be fulfilled."

"Can't it? They just said you had to go on the date. They didn't say with whom."

Jen took tentative steps toward the table, a tray with two dinner plates in her hand. Drew waved her over.

I speared Drew with a look. "I'm not going on a date with you."

"Of course not." He said it like the idea was preposterous. "But I'm pretty sure you can eat a meal with me to get your beloved donation."

Jen practically tossed the plates on the table before retreating. Poor girl. I'd have to leave her a hefty tip for all the chaos she'd endured. I touched her arm and asked for the check before she scurried all the way back to the kitchen.

"My friends will see reason," I pointed out to Drew.

He picked up the knife sitting at an angle along the edge of the plate and cut David's burger in half. "Will they?"

Something in his tone caused me to pause. "Are you...blackmailing me?" I gaped at him, gathering my thoughts before I continued. "If I don't sit down and eat with you, then you'll somehow sabotage this donation? Do you hate the planet that much?"

He picked up the burger and took a bite, making appreciative noises in the back of his throat. He held the burger up. "This is really good. You want a bite?"

I sat back down in my chair with a thud. "Did you know that seventy percent of all agricultural land is used to raise farm animals? A lot of that is for grazing, which could be used to grow crops for human consumption. Livestock farming also leads to deforestation in key places like the Amazon and is a major component of the loss of biodiversity."

He studied the hamburger in his hand. "So you're saying my dinner is at the epicenter of world hunger and basically the end of the natural world as we know it?" He stared right into my eyes as he took a huge bite. "What a delicious way to go," he said around a mouthful of food.

"You're a horrible person." I stabbed at a piece of romaine lettuce with my fork.

"Awwww. I'm sure you say that to all the guys."

A cherry tomato died at the end of my fork tines. "Why are you here?"

He wiped his mouth and lifted a fry. "I thought it was pretty obvious." He popped the fried potato wedge in his mouth. "I'm eating dinner."

A cucumber succumbed to my silverware attack. "No. Why are you *here?*"

He looked right at me and repeated slowly, "I thought it was pretty obvious."

Obvious to whom? The need to reduce the human carbon footprint was obvious. The need for social reforms was obvious. Why a man I couldn't stand and who had made his mocking regard of me evident chose to not only eat with me but blackmail me to do so was about as clear as a mud puddle.

"How's Sierra?"

His jump in topic and the casual way he brought my daughter into conversation left me reeling. "Pardon?"

His brow quirked. "Your daughter? Eight years old, about this high"—he motioned with his hand—"and too smart for her own good."

"I know who my daughter is."

He shrugged. "You seemed confused."

My molars ground together. "She's fine."

"Still playing soccer?"

I pushed down the queasiness in my gut. Sierra didn't get her athletic prowess from me. And as much as I encouraged her to put her energy into debate club and her chess team, she'd still managed to talk me into signing her up for team sports. Stupid debate club coming back to bite me on the behind.

It took all my will to remove the anxious tension I felt when I pictured my daughter padded up and on the field. "No. She decided she wanted to try football."

"Flag?"

"Tackle."

Drew blanched. "But the league here is co-ed with a high majority of players being boys." He said it as if I weren't aware of the ramifications.

I bristled at his tone. "And I'm not raising a wilting daisy."

He studied me, thoughts skimming across his face, never settling long enough for me to get a read. "What made you so…"

"Dramatic?" The word punched out my lungs.

He shook his head slowly, almost as if my word choice saddened him. "I was going to say passionate."

Passionate sounded…nice? But that couldn't be right. In the months I'd been acquainted with Drew, he'd never said a nice thing to me. No, his M.O. was to see how many of my buttons he could push. He got some sick satisfaction in working me up into a tizzy. I told myself repeatedly not to rise to his bait, but there were a few (okay, a lot) of issues I refused to stay silent on. Which meant passionate to me—me caring enough about things to fight for them—but probably meant something different to him. A wild, unbalanced harridan with too much zeal and not enough self-control.

"I only seem passionate because you look at the world through a lens of apathy."

His jaw clenched then released. A low chuckle rumbled through his chest and he stood. "Come on. We've eaten and discussed three topics. Let me walk you to your car so you can collect your money."

He threw a one hundred dollar bill on the table while I stood. If he thought I'd let him pay and somehow be indebted to him, he had another thing coming. I opened my purse, but a hand closed around the opening.

"Don't." All playfulness vanished from his eyes, and they seemed to darken somehow. "I can't make that guy take back the lies he said to you—and they *were* lies, Nicole—but I can prevent him from heaping insult on top of injury by taking care of the check and tip."

Where had the immature version of Drew gone? Who was this man in his place? Shocked from an argument, I nodded in agreement. He placed his hand on the small of my back, the pressure reigniting my brainwaves enough to have the mental acumen to move away from his touch.

I couldn't see his grin but felt it thickening between us.

"Is this you?" He nodded to my pale-blue electric car with the *Save the chubby unicorns* bumper sticker outlining a white rhino.

I pressed the button on my key fob to unlock the doors.

"For our next date, I'll pick you up in my SUV. It might use more gas, but at least it wasn't made on the backs of child labor in cobalt mines." He turned and started to walk away.

"I'm not going... My car wasn't..." I sputtered, his mocking laugh echoing in my ears.

Crime-a-nitally, I really hated that guy.

Nicole Applegate was one infuriating woman. Ninety percent of the time I wanted to shake some sense out of her. Yes, out. (She had way too much for her own good.) The other ten percent, I thought it would be a better idea to kiss her senseless. Either way, I one hundred percent thought she needed to relax a bit more.

She was as tightly wound as violin strings. Don't get me wrong. I enjoyed plucking those tight strings and hearing her sing. And man, could she let out a full concerto on the right topic. But the woman never rested. If she wasn't careful, all those beautiful strings were going to snap, then all she'd be left with was a gorgeously-shaped piece of wood. Elegant curves and all.

No hum of an internal combustion engine announced the car pulling up to the stop sign beside me. I paused at The Loft's entrance and turned to see Nicole behind the wheel of her *green machine*. I had no idea if she called her electric car that, but remembering the outrage in her cobalt-blue eyes when I accused her vehicle of supporting child mining made my lips turn up.

I stared at her through the driver's side window. No way she couldn't feel someone's eyes on her. Her fingers gripped the steering wheel, but she stubbornly refused to turn her head and look at me. Once the car with right of way at the four-way stop passed the intersection, Nicole accelerated like a turtle—although I bet she wished she had some horses under that hood that could peel away with rubber burning—and left me in a cloud of dust only seen in her imagination.

I chuckled, shook my head, and opened the front door to the restaurant. I'd been at the bar waiting for a to-go order when I'd overheard Nicole and jerkface's conversation. I'd wanted to haul him out of the restaurant by the back of the collar and banish him and his not-so-subtle jab at Nicole's figure. Then maybe I'd do him a favor and toss the card of one of my optometrist friends at him, because he was obviously blind. Nicole may've had a sharp tongue, but she was soft in ways that made a man entertain thoughts he shouldn't.

Like kissing her senseless ten percent of the time.

"Ready for your order?" the bartender asked when he noticed my presence.

"Yes. Thank you." He slipped to the back and

returned with a large paper bag. I handed him a five dollar bill as a tip, took the food, and left.

My Suburban thrummed to life, and I put my hand on the dash, feeling the vibrations of the engine through my fingertips. Nicole would probably love to dump a bucket of pine sap down my pants for driving this fossil fuel guzzler. The thought made me press down on the accelerator and rev the engine.

Throwing the SUV into gear, I pulled out of the parking lot and took back roads to avoid construction traffic. The highway could get more backed up than plumbing in a frat house. Two things I knew to avoid.

Ten minutes later, I pulled into the driveway of my sister's mid-century modern home. There weren't many places geographically where a house with a flat roof didn't spell disaster, but Southern California was one of them. Three panels of overlarge windows offset the dark siding. The front door opened, and my sister Ginny stepped out, arms crossed over her protruding belly.

"Andrew Bauer, you'd think you'd be smart enough not to keep a pregnant woman waiting for food."

I cupped my hand behind my ear and shut the Suburban's door. "What was that? Thank you for going out of your way to pick up dinner for me? But of course, dear sister. Anything for you."

Ginny swatted my shoulder when I came close enough, then peeked in the bag. "Did you remember extra pickles?"

I walked past her into the kitchen and set the bag on the table. "And a whole lemon quartered for you. I should get extra brother credits for that one. You know the looks I got from the woman taking my order?"

Ginny ignored me and pulled out a container, popped the lid, then placed a lemon wedge between her teeth. "Stop keeping score."

"How else am I supposed to prove I'm the best brother on the planet?"

She tossed the yellow rind in the trash. "This doesn't even begin to make up for some of the things you did to me when we were kids."

"I was an angel."

She snorted. "Yeah. Of the one-third variety that got kicked out of heaven."

I grinned and ducked when a lemon wedge flew at my head.

"I'm scared of dark, tight spaces because you used to put a bean bag on my head and sit on it!"

"Classic. Speaking of big brothers, where's Owen? Uncle Drew needs to impart some wisdom. He has a lot to learn before urchin number two arrives." I pointed to Ginny's stomach.

She glared at me but her lips twitched. "Stop calling my darling offspring urchins. And Owen's in the back-yard throwing the football with Eric."

Ginny returned to pulling food out of the restaurant's disposable containers, so I moved to the sliding glass door that led to the backyard.

"This time I want you to run a quick slant route." Eric, Ginny's husband, had his head down beside their nine-year-old son in a two-man huddle. "Ready?"

Owen moved down the invisible line and crouched into a runner's starting position. "Ready."

"Hike," Eric called, falling back a few pivots and cocking the ball, ready to throw.

Owen sprinted forward, then turned to run a forty-five-degree angle toward the middle of the "field." Eric tossed the ball, and it landed in Owen's arms with a soft thud.

"Touchdown!" I yelled, hands thrown up like a ref making the call. "Now, where's that victory dance I taught you?" With one hand on the back of my neck and the other gripping an ankle, I started pumping. Up, down. Back and forth. I let go and crossed my wrists in front of me, galloping in a tight circle like I was riding a horse. Finally, I ended in a muscle man pose, left arm extended out front, right arm curled behind me, flexing my not-NFL-grade muscles for all they were worth.

"Excessive celebration." Eric booed. "Fifteen-yard penalty."

I laughed and hooked an elbow around my nephew's neck, pulling him to my side. He looked up at me with a wide smile, and I winked down at him. "Totally worth sharing my awesome moves with the world though, am I right?"

He patted my shoulder. "Sure, Uncle Drew. You keep telling yourself that."

I tried to replicate the look Ginny and Eric shared so often over their son's head. The one that said *Where'd this kid come from and what happened to my sweet baby boy?* "Where'd he pick up the sass mouth?"

Eric's brows hiked. "I believe that would be from his uncle."

"Oh." I ran my knuckles over Owen's head. "In that case, keep up the good work."

He swatted my hand away. "Is it safe to go inside yet?"

My questioning gaze shot to Eric. He picked the football off the ground and tossed it between his hands.

"You know how hard the third trimester can be."

"No, he doesn't." Ginny appeared in the doorway. "No man can ever know until all their organs are squished together, they have a watermelon constantly kicking them from the inside, and their ankles decide to see if they have what it takes to moonlight as water balloons."

We three males stared at each other, not daring to utter a word. Ginny may've been exhibiting signs of a spitfire, but the tide could change and waterworks be turned on at any minute.

Eric looked past me—the martyr—and his eyes softened the moment they landed on his wife.

Emotion started to collect in my throat. Grief. Longing. Nothing I wanted to face or entertain.

Time for an eviction notice.

I caught Owen's eyes and winked. "Don't worry. I fed the beast."

Owen snickered.

Something like a growl came from the direction of the house. "I'll pretend I didn't hear that since you brought me chocolate lava cake." Ginny harrumphed. "All right. Everyone wash up. I've got the food set out on the table." Owen and Eric filed past her, but Ginny set a hand on my arm when I moved to do the same. "Not sure if you were planning to stay, but I put your dinner on a plate too."

I scratched my jaw. "I, uh, already ate actually."

She tilted her head. "Then who was the grilled salmon for?"

I moved past her, careful not to bump her stomach. "Me."

She slid the door shut and marched to close the distance I'd put between us. "But you've already eaten?" Suspicion and interest laced her question. "Is that why you were late?"

"I was helping a damsel in distress."

Eric made a disbelieving sound. "More like distressing a damsel."

Nicole's hard jaw and fiery eyes flashed through my mind. Yeah, that was probably more accurate.

Ginny saw my grin and rolled her eyes. "Men."

Eric sidled behind her and wrapped his arms around her waist, caressing her round belly while placing delicate kisses down her neck. "Now, babe, you know you wouldn't want to live without us."

Ginny let out a contented sigh and leaned back in Eric's arms.

That would've been my cue to vamoose if something Nicole had said hadn't put me on alert. Before I left, I needed to check to make sure. The odds were low, but still.

Funny thing was, I didn't know what answer I hoped for.

"Hey, Eric."

My brother-in-law lazily lifted his head from his wife's neck. "Hmm?"

"Can I see the team roster again? I want to check something."

"Sure. I meant to forward it to you anyway, Coach. You'll need it before next week." He dug his phone out of his pocket and tapped the screen a few times. A minute later, my phone dinged its email notification. I tapped the app icon and opened the email, quickly scanning the list of names. My eyes froze on the second to last.

Sierra Applegate.

I bit down on my lips to keep them from spreading into a smile.

Looked like Nicole and I were about to be spending a lot more time together.

3

NICOLE

*T*he low murmur of voices, punctuated by a laugh here and there, drifted through the living room wall of Molly and Jocelyn's Spanish-style house to reach me in the kitchen. I pinched a bit of wheatgrass between my fingers and garnished the top of the last glass. *There.* No hidden surprise ingredients this time—although, the black bean brownie and tofu cheesecake were both delicious, so I didn't know what the girls were complaining about—and I hadn't bent to the peer pressure of their toxic taste buds.

I gripped the handles of the tray laden with five full glasses and slipped out of the kitchen to join my friends. Tonight was sewing night, but a quick glance around the room proved my suspicions correct. Not a single pair of Fiskars scissors had been removed from a bag, much less fabric, patterns, or needles. It wouldn't stay that way. Jocelyn needed to work on Molly's wedding dress, after all, and the rest of us had been tasked with bridesmaid and flower girl creations. But for the moment, we'd all sip the mocktails I'd made and simply breathe. Maybe I could remind them of the donation they'd promised without getting grilled on the details of the date.

Hey, a girl could dream, couldn't she?

Amanda's nose wrinkled as she eyed the tray in my hand. "What's that?"

I slid the tray onto the coffee table. "Refreshments."

"I vote Molly take the first sip and tell us how it is." Betsy pushed her thick curls off her shoulder.

Molly had a strict honesty policy. A compulsion, really. She'd gotten a bit better since being with Ben, but she still adhered to the truth as if she'd bathed in Elmer's school glue.

Molly reached for a glass and brought it closer to her face to inspect. "What's ummm…"—she picked out a blade of wheatgrass from the dairy-free whipped cream—"this…garnish?"

Betsy cackled. "Did you get that from the lawn mower bag?"

I placed my hands on my hips. "It's wheatgrass, and it's very good for you. Excuse me for loving you guys so much that I want to keep you healthy."

"Malachi would call that cow food." Jocelyn smiled. Malachi, her boyfriend, owned and operated a dude ranch. She'd met him when her company held their corporate retreat at his property. She hadn't even seen a horse in real life before that, but now she was on her way to becoming the most Boho-chic cowgirl on the west coast.

Condensation from the glass moistened my hand as I curled my fingers around the side. I took a long pull, sweet carrot juice and creamy coconut milk sliding down my throat. Smacking my lips together, I said, "They're called Peter Rabbit mocktails, and they're delicious."

The girls still stared dubiously at the orange drinks as if I might have served them poison.

I rolled my eyes and picked the tray back up. "Fine. Let me pop a can of battery acid dissolver, and you guys can slowly rot from the inside out."

Amanda stopped me with a hand on my arm. She licked her lips. "Wheatgrass, huh? Some of the Stampeder players drink shots of that." She lifted one of the glasses like it was a champagne flute at a party. She tentatively brought the white coconut cream to her mouth and tipped the glass ever so slightly. Her eyes widened. "It almost tastes like carrot cake."

Jocelyn held out her hand. "Give me the livestock munchies."

I passed around the drinks. "Maybe next time I offer you sustenance, you won't balk so much."

Molly met my gaze. "I think our blind acceptance of food from your hand went out the window when you made me eat Pinocchio's conscience."

"Cricket flour is more sustainable—" I cut myself

off. "You know what? You don't have to worry about that since I'm vegan now."

"Not *that* anyway." Betsy removed all traces of green from her drink.

"With friends like you guys…"

Amanda hooked her arm around my neck, pressing her temple to mine. "You know we love you."

"Uh huh."

Molly clapped her hands together. "All right. Enough of this chit chat, ladies. My wedding is in six weeks, and these dresses won't make themselves."

Like the fabled bunny chased by Mr. McGregor, the Peter Rabbit mocktails were soon out of sight.

Jocelyn pulled some white cotton-blend material from a canvas bag and started unfolding pieces while Betsy retrieved the dress form she'd made.

A few weeks prior, she'd instructed Molly to don form-fitting undergarments and an extra-long T-shirt. Then the duct tape wrapping had begun. A layer for the body casting, around and around, but after three layers of tape, she had a form. Molly could barely bend to show her waistline, but no one wanted a waistless dress —plus how would Jocelyn know where to put the cute little bow in her design?—so bend Molly did. Betsy had finally cut Molly out of the duct tape with a snipped line up her back.

The dress form took center stage. A headless silver encasement of Molly's body. Jocelyn unfolded the top piece of cut material, and I grabbed a container of straight pins and held them out to her. With deft movements, she smoothed the material over the form's bust and started pining. She cut a line up from the waist, added more material, and pinned again, creating darts in the bodice of the dress. She snipped notches into the bottom of the pattern pieces to make sure they lay flat, then smoothed excess into the side seam. After a while, she took a black marker and made dots along the fabric.

"What are those for?" Betsy asked. She and Amanda weren't really sewers, but they were handy for unpicking seams and cutting out patterns.

"I'm just marking the neckline," Jocelyn answered. Her design had been pinned to a cork board along with other wedding ideas we'd cut out from magazines. Cakes, flowers, invitations, etc.

"Have I told you how much I love your design?" Molly asked.

One side of Jocelyn's lips hitched. "Only every day." She kept marking the side seam and baseline for future alignment.

Jocelyn's eye for design had been a hidden talent only recently discovered—a childhood dream she'd set aside for more adult responsibilities and financial stability. If it hadn't been for her shy cowboy, we might have never been privy to her talent.

The dress she'd designed for Molly wasn't only gorgeous but embodied her personality as well. Simple, elegant, and honest. The wide bateau neckline would showcase Molly's graceful neck and collar bones. The trimmed waist and bow spoke to her sense of whimsy. We all agreed, however, that the fuller side panels that arched just below her hips held the pièce de résistance within their folds: pockets.

So different than my own wedding dress had been. Instead of friends coming together to shower me with love, bonding over the work of our hands and dreaming of the future together, I'd only had my mother and her ability to put everything into a global perspective. So when she pointed out I could either have the dress of my dreams or use that money for a greater good that would have a far more lasting impact than a single day, I walked out of the bridal boutique with a heavily discounted gown due to the beading turning yellow, a dirty hemline, and a small tear under the armpit. The mermaid silhouette had done nothing for my figure, and I'd been self-conscious of my extra curves being hugged so tightly on my wedding day.

But the money I'd saved had gone to purchase a small herd of goats for an African village, and as my mother liked to point out, hadn't that been the wiser choice, since the goats continued to make a difference while my marriage had been an epic failure?

Jocelyn retrieved her best pair of scissors and cut along the lines she'd marked. Amanda groaned loud and long.

"What?" Jocelyn's hand stilled and she inspected the pattern. "What's wrong?"

"Oh. Sorry, it's not that." Amanda lifted her phone from her lap and waved it around a little. "Something with work."

Jocelyn and Molly exhaled simultaneously. Jocelyn started cutting again.

A few minutes later, Amanda let out a sigh and cradled her head in her hands.

"*Ay probecita.*" Betsy clucked her tongue. "Is one of your players getting traded or something?"

Amanda worked as a social media public relations manager in the sports world but was currently contracted with the baseball team, the Stampeders. A trade wouldn't have her sighing and moaning like she was about to pass a kidney stone.

"What's wrong?" I asked.

She bit her lip, staring at the phone's screen. She didn't appear to have heard me, so I asked again.

Almost as if it pained her, she set the her phone on her leg and looked up.

"One of our relief pitchers, Dennis Nichols, took a knee during the national anthem. Social media is blowing up over it, and the team's owner is demanding I Band-aid the gushing wound."

"I thought kneeling during the anthem was more of a football thing," Betsy said, brows scrunched together.

I found another container of straight pins for Jocelyn. "No, it's more of a human rights thing." Not that half the nation agreed with me on that point.

Amanda picked her phone back up and tapped the

screen. "Well, according to a lot of the outraged comments online, it's being perceived as a lack of respect thing. Especially for the service members who've made the ultimate sacrifice for this country."

"Your dad's in the Navy, Molly. What does he think about people taking a knee during the anthem as a means to protest systemic racism?" Betsy asked.

Molly peered out the window. Her parents had had a change of duty assignment in the spring and were now stationed overseas in Japan. She hadn't seen them since they left. "Those who've served in the military seem to be as split on the issue as the rest of the country. Personally, Dad says he fights and sacrifices for *all* rights for *all* Americans. That includes the right to freedom of speech and the right to protest. These players are using the platform they have to peacefully bring public attention to a real problem in our country. I think, most of all, that he's sad that anyone would even *need* to take a stand—or kneel, rather—because of inequality in this day and age. But he says the fact these players kneel doesn't feel like a personal slap in the face to him. Then again, there are people in the service that do feel like their sacrifice isn't appreciated by such actions so..." She shrugged helplessly. "It's a trigger topic, isn't it?"

"Maybe when the police stop kneeling on the necks of our men, killing them when they aren't so much as struggling, then the players won't feel they have to kneel during the anthem anymore." Jocelyn's voice broke, and she wiped a tear away with a shaky hand. She inhaled a trembling breath, looked up at the ceiling, and blinked rapidly. "Sorry," she choked out.

Molly wrapped her arms around Jocelyn's shoulders. "Are you okay?"

"Yeah, sorry." Jocelyn shook out her wrists. "My brother called last night. A couple of days ago he was out jogging when two police officers came out of nowhere and wrestled him to the ground. Apparently a call about a car robbery in the area came in, and he fit the description of the suspect."

We were all quiet, no doubt imagining how scary such a thing would be. To just be out taking a jog, then all of a sudden violently brought down by police officers for no apparent reason.

"I know they were just trying to do their jobs, but they could have asked for his license and questioned him before automatically painting him a criminal and handcuffing him for simply exercising. This happens too often, and my heart is tired and hurting because of it. I mean, a Black man can't even drive a nice car without someone assuming he stole it." Her shoulders rose. "My head knows the majority of the men and women who put on the black and blue uniforms have done so because they want to protect and serve, but it's so hard when things like this, and even worse things, happen every day because of the pigment of a person's skin. It's just...the system..."

Her voice trailed because, really, what was there to say?

"You know what we need?" Molly asked brightly, looking straight at me.

An uneasy wave curled in my belly. "More Peter Rabbit mocktails?"

"A happier topic. Tell us how your date went."

"That would *not* be a happier topic." My insides churned.

Amanda curled her legs under her. "Spill. We're dying to know."

I made a show of looking at my wristwatch. "Oh, look at that. I need to go relieve my babysitter."

"No worries," Molly said, nonplussed. "I'll fill them in."

Amanda gasped and leaned forward. "What do you know?"

That wave of unease tumbled me like a newbie surfer.

Molly grinned. "Ben told me."

"I'm confused," Betsy interjected. "How would Ben know how Nicole's date went?"

"From Drew." Molly's eyes held mine captive, probing their depths to gauge my reaction.

"And Drew would know because…" Jocelyn let the sentence dangle.

I finally broke Molly's gaze. "Because the date ended up being with him." My eyes landed on each of my friends. "But you all can wipe those looks off your faces. You'd have better odds of logging companies implementing reforestation in the Amazon than Drew and me ever developing romantic feelings for each other."

Case closed.

The end. Or so I hoped.

4

DREW

I'd learned early on in medical school to utilize any spare minute I could find. Waiting at the DMV to renew my license? Perfect for studying flash cards on infant diseases. Waiting for a movie to begin in the theater? Time to review my notes from the guest lecturer from John Hopkins. Now those spare moments looked more like grabbing a power bar between patients or shooting off a text to my sister to remind her to take her prenatal vitamins.

I sat in my Suburban, windows down, and glanced at the digital clock on the dashboard. Ten minutes before practice began. Eric tossed the football to Owen in the field across the street. A kid and his mom walked along the green from the opposite side.

I lifted my phone from the cup holder and held it up in front of me so face recognition could unlock the screen. The hospital discouraged us from giving out our personal numbers—stressed those boundaries for legal and ethical reasons as well as to establish healthy limits for their residents. But sometimes a patient would enter the exam room that needed a little extra assurance and care. A pregnant teen alone, scared. No support from the father or her parents. Or the single mother with dark circles under her eyes, worried about her son or daughter but also wondering how she'll pay the medical bills.

Occasionally, when I met a patient like that, I'd write my number on a pad and slip the paper into their palm with the reassurance that they could call me day or night. Most never did, but sometimes I'd get a text or voicemail with a concern that I could easily respond to and assuage their fears.

Such a text sat in my messenger app. I tapped the white speech bubble icon and read the few short sentences again. Nothing to be too concerned over, and I was glad I could put this mother's current fears to rest.

A car slowly passed on my side, red brake light glowing. The smaller white backup lights followed a second later. Parallel parking? Most people would drive around the block until they found an easier parking spot.

I tapped out a response on my phone, glancing up every other word, hoping the driver of the electric car knew how to wedge the small vehicle into the bookended space. With precision, the back fender angled closer to me. Then the lights went off and the front end eased forward.

Something about the car tickled at my memory...

The passenger side back door swung open, and out popped a familiar face. Similar to her mother, Sierra Applegate had a slightly square jaw and a knowing glint to her eyes. I hadn't spent a lot of time with her, but she struck me as someone a bit too serious for only having experienced eight years of life. The times I'd been in her presence, I'd expected her to prattle on about new mods on Minecraft or her favorite YouTuber. Instead, I'd gotten an exposé on the dangers the kelp forests off our shores faced and a rundown on how to capture an opponent's king with the minimum number of plays in chess.

Nicole stepped out on the driver's side, a phone pressed to her ear.

Then again, maybe I shouldn't have been so surprised, given who Sierra's mom was. Someone needed to teach both mother and daughter how to loosen up, live a little, and have some fun. Maybe football could do that for Sierra, but what would it take for Nicole to stop playing at Atlas and remove the weight of the world from her shoulders?

Nicole bent down and reached into the car, then the trunk popped open a few inches. She came around the back.

"Hold on a second, Mama." She pulled the phone

away from her ear to talk to Sierra. "Do you have your mouthguard?"

I'd originally rolled the windows down to catch a nice breeze, but this was a nice bonus.

Sierra spread her lips to reveal a black guard protecting her teeth.

Nicole nodded once. "Okay, go ahead to the field and meet your team, and I'll be there in a minute with your pads."

Sierra looked both ways before sprinting across the street and making a beeline to Eric on the field. I should probably head over there myself...in a minute.

I pressed send on my text as Nicole lifted her trunk open and set her phone on the lip.

"All right, Mama. I'm back."

"How many times have I told you not to call me that?" a voice scolded over the speaker. "My identity isn't wrapped up in a role, and I'd appreciate it if you'd call me by the name on my birth certificate."

Nicole massage her forehead. "You can be Shirley to everyone else, *Mama*." She emphasized the last word.

A loud sigh crackled over the connection. "As I was saying, your brother Barritt's testimony clinched the victory in court yesterday. The Navy can no longer detonate their ship shock explosives in Southern California waters. You know how many endangered whales, dolphins, and seals he saved from death and injury?"

Nicole moved things around in her trunk. "That's great, Mama."

I felt my brows climb to my hairline. The words were right, but they lacked any sort of conviction. And who was this version of Nicole that didn't get convicted about the state of the planet? She should be pumping her fists over saving endangered whales, not mindlessly shuffling stuff around in her trunk like she didn't live and breathe environmental causes.

A better man wouldn't eavesdrop. But then again, I'd never been called a better man. I slouched down in my seat behind the wheel in case Nicole turned around and spotted me.

"Have you talked to your sister lately? Her case against ICE and the detention centers is really making headlines. She's getting the attention of some important people over at Amnesty International."

"Mm-hmm."

"But enough about your siblings. What about you? What have you done lately to make this a better world to live in?"

Nicole gripped the open trunk lid and let her temple rest on her right arm. Her thick brown hair had been twisted up and pinned to her head in some way so that her long neck was exposed. The muscles on either side of her spine corded, tension mapping its way through her body with every word projected out of the phone's speaker. She sighed, and her left arm fell to her side, limp in defeat. "Mama, I can't do this right now. Sierra is about to start her first football practice, and I need to get her pads to her."

"Football!" Shirley's appalled response would've better followed a declaration of an impending drug deal, not a youth sports event. "Nicole, what are you thinking? These Neanderthal games are nothing more than auction blocks for human trafficking. That you would put my granddaughter—"

"*My* daughter, Mama. And she's waiting for me, so I've got to go." Nicole fingered the phone with enough force to break a phalange.

I opened my door and shut it quietly behind me. "I see where you get it now."

Nicole started and spun around. "Drew? What are you doing here?"

I ignored her question. "Your passion, I mean."

Nicole eyed her phone like it would leap out and bite her. "My mother and I are nothing alike."

My hands dug to the bottom of my pockets, and I leaned against the front fender of the Suburban. "Maybe not. But it's hard to thrive under that type of..." I searched for the right word. "...expectation."

She snorted and turned back to her open trunk, wrestling with a filled trash bag.

I pushed off my vehicle and stepped beside her. "Here." I took the bag from her, pulling gently since the edge seemed to be caught on a metal hinge and I didn't want the thin plastic to rip. As I worked the side loose, the closure opened and I peeked inside. "Is that…" I blinked, but nothing changed.

She grabbed the orange strings of the closure and pulled tight.

"What are you doing with bags full of human hair? Planning to frame someone for a few hundred crimes with all this DNA evidence?"

"Don't be ridiculous," she muttered under her breath.

"You're donating the leftover locks to a doll maker so they can make even creepier nightmare inspirations?"

She eyed me, then pushed the bag farther back, exposing a set of youth-sized shoulder pads. I grabbed the neck and yanked, dislodging and freeing the equipment.

"If you're not donating, then maybe you're hoping to sell the strands in a heroic and selfless act for a beloved family member."

Nicole barked out one staccato note of laughter. Sharp but full. A single sound that seemed to have emerged on the air victorious. Free from the captivity of being held in.

My chest swelled. I'd heard Nicole laugh before. She wasn't always dour-faced and somber. She smiled with her friends, and her joy could float on the breeze like the trill of a flautist. But this was the first note of the first measure that I'd had a part in playing.

"The hair would all have to be mine to be a selfless

act, wouldn't it? And for that to be true, I'd have to grow my hair out and shave it a few dozen times to get this amount." She shook her head. "I don't know where you come up with half the things that come out of your mouth."

"I can't take the credit for this one. That was all Jo from *Little Women*."

"You know *Little Women*?"

I shrugged. "I have a sister."

She looked over her shoulder at the field, and my eyes followed her gaze. Eric had the team in a circle around him. Introductions had already started. I really should head over there.

A tug on the pads in my hands brought my focus back to Nicole.

"Thanks for your help, but I need to get these to Sierra."

I tightened my grip. "Not so fast. I still need to hear about why you have bags of human hair in your trunk. Very suspicious, Miss Applegate, and as a good citizen, it's my duty to report suspicious behavior."

Her full lips turned down. "Let go, Drew."

I met her glare with an impish one of my own. "Tell me about the hair, Nicole."

She half-growled, half-sighed as she folded her arms over her chest. "Fine. I gather all the swept up clippings at the studio where I work and store them until they're needed."

"When are the offcuts of human hair, collected from hair stylists, ever needed?"

"When disaster strikes oil rigs and spills thousands of gallons of crude oil into the water, killing marine life and polluting habitats."

She was saving hair...to clean up oil spills... "Hair?" My voice sounded incredulous to my own ears.

She rolled her eyes. "Yes, hair. Human hair is hydrophobic and biosorbent, which means it both repels water and collects heavy metals and other contaminants, like oil. It's natural, reusable, and the cutoffs only go to landfill anyway."

My fingers loosened around the football pads. "Wow. I never would have thought of that."

She reached forward and snatched Sierra's equipment from my limp grip. "Yeah, well, I didn't think of it either. Just read about someone else's research."

"And then put the idea into action. Wait, is the fact the hypothesis didn't originate with you why you didn't tell your mom about your hair-hoarding-to-save-the-oceans practice?"

This time her laugh was brittle. "*Shirley* would not see sweeping up and storing hair clippings as anything noteworthy, trust me."

"So you're not a tree hugger on steroids for your mom's approval, and you obviously don't mind getting in her craw if the amount of times you emphasized the word *mama* says anything."

A ghost of a smile passed over Nicole's lips.

"So tell me, what is the drive behind your Captain Planet superhero persona?"

She shut the trunk and locked her car with the press of a button on her key fob. Her gaze rose to mine and bore in. Studying me as if I confused her.

"No one has asked me that in a long time," she said in a quiet voice. "They just assume I'm a liberal fanatic. So much granola going to my brain that I care more about ecology than economy."

"But that's not the case?"

A car whizzed past, the displaced air ruffling Nicole's hair. A strand fell from the confines of her updo and brushed her cheek.

"I'm a Christian."

Three words. A declaration. As if those three words said everything.

Unfortunately, that cleared everything up about as well as an Alka-Seltzer tablet dissolving in water. "I know Christians who think climate change is all a hoax or a conspiracy theory, so you're going to have to give me more than that."

Nicole checked for traffic before stepping out to cross the street. I followed at her side.

"In Genesis, God gave man dominion over the Earth. Some people take that to mean Earth's natural resources are ours to exploit."

"But you don't." I had to admit, I'd never really considered the wording of the verse before.

"No. God spent six days creating beautiful, imaginative things. From an atmosphere that gives us dazzling sunsets that challenge artists, to plants that can photosynthesize and use the sun He set in the sky to produce their own food. From the smallest insect to the greatest mammal, He designed every cell to work in unison, knowing the beginning and the end and hardwiring adaptations into His models. And then He made man in His own image. And bestowed on him dominion over all His creation. That's power, sure, but we should all be humbled by the responsibility on our shoulders. To not only care for but nurture everything He spoke, touched, and breathed life into. From the great oceans to the tiniest speck of algae. From the giant animals that roam the grasslands to the smallest arthropod in the jungles. Not to mention the one created being He formed with His own hand. Bent down and breathed life into sculpted lungs." She looked away and retuned a wave from Sierra. "I'm just trying to do the part that God has asked me to do."

Silence overtook me as I tried to process the depth of her conviction. I never would have guessed her motivation was driven by a sacred sense of Christian duty.

"And now it's my turn to ask you a question."

I raised my eyes to hers.

"What are you doing here?"

The same thing she'd asked me at the restaurant.

I pulled a whistle out of my pocket and twirled it in

a wide circle beside my body. I caught it midair, brought it to my lips, and blew. Turning to the group of kids staring wide-eyed at me, I shouted, "Who's ready to play some football?"

5

NICOLE

*O*f all the youth football teams in all the towns in all the world, he had to coach Sierra's.

I looked up at the sky, a fluffy white cloud lazily floating along the blue expanse over my head, and mouthed, *Really?* Evidence what it was, I believed God had a sense of humor. But I *didn't* think He got His kicks at the expense of His children. Even so, I would've sworn I heard a deep, throaty chuckle that danced on the breeze my direction, swirling around me and leaving me almost dizzy. The sound was pleasant. Rich, like a salted-caramel, double-chocolate lava cake, the gooey center oozing around me until the last strands were carried away.

I blinked up at the sky. Tilted my ear. Another laugh, but the divine cadence hadn't come from the heavens. The earthly origination pulled my face back toward the field. Drew lunged for one of the players on his team, and the boy jumped to the side and ran away.

Drew chuckled. "I almost had you that time, Weston."

Internally, I sent another *Really?* skyward, collected all the warm gooeyness Drew's laugh had elicited, and shoved it to a corner to solidify into a hard chocolate rock.

Maybe our being thrown together so often wasn't so much a cosmic joke as it was a test, my patience and tolerance being thrust center stage with a spotlight beaming down, exposing every angle. I sighed, knowing I'd failed thus far. But there was just something about the man that got under my skin.

"You didn't tell me Dr. Swoony number two was Sierra's coach."

I jumped and spun, my hand going to cover my pounding heart. Amanda's pert lips sported a mischievous smile as she swayed back on her heels, her hands inserted into her back pockets.

I pushed on her shoulder, knocking her off balance so she had to take a step back. "Don't sneak up on a person like that."

Her grin widened. "I didn't sneak. You were staring off into space. Or at your daughter's coach, rather." She waggled her eyebrows.

I bit the inside of my bottom lip. A denial would only be fuel to her teasing.

"None of my coaches were that hot when I played

sports. Do you think Sierra's going to develop a little crush on him?"

My eyes bugged out. "She's eight."

Amanda's lips rolled between her teeth, her attempt at hiding her amusement at my expense failing miserably. "How old were you when you had your first crush?"

Warning sirens blared against my ear drums, my mind starting a lockdown sequence against the memory. Too late. I saw him in my mind's eye. Blake Turner. Hair parted down the middle with waves on both sides, the ends looping to rest near the corners of his eyes Jonathan Taylor Thomas-style. I was seven and he was two years older and my brother's best friend. Nothing had ever happened between us, even though I fancied myself in love. Might have even written our names together and drawn a heart around them.

"Exactly," Amanda crowed.

My neck heated. "But that's different. Maybe Sierra will like one of her teammates, but Drew is a grown man."

The skin around Amanda's eyes pinched, but whatever had been there quickly vanished. She shimmied her shoulders in her stilted way. "Trust me. I've noticed."

I pushed her shoulder again. "You're really bad sometimes, you know that?"

The step back she took seemed to jar her, but she smiled even bigger. "And you're so busy being good all the time that you miss out on a lot of fun. Maybe you should try it my way for once."

I shook my head. "No, thank you."

A flat ladder-looking thing had been laid out on the ground. Kids lined up behind it and took turns doing some kind of footwork through the rungs. In the middle, to the left. In the middle, to the right. If I tried to mimic their movements, I'd trip all over my feet and end up flat on my face.

Sierra stepped up, her knees rising and falling quickly as she worked her way to the end, her ponytail swaying back and forth. She seemed focused and determined, and I told myself to relax. The possibility of injury—especially head injuries—caused me all kinds of anxiety, but I couldn't let my worries leach out and infect my daughter.

"She looks good." Amanda spoke at my side, her focus also now on the players instead of their coach.

Sierra toed over the last rung, and I glanced back at Amanda. "What are you doing here, anyway? I thought you'd be busy putting out the fires started by Dennis Nichols and his silent protest."

Amanda's exhale almost sounded of defeat. "Not sure what's going to be salvageable when the flames die down." She nodded to the field. "I needed to get out of the smoke. Remind myself what the love of the game feels like."

"Sorry things at work have been tough lately."

She shrugged. "That's life I guess, right? Sometimes

it can knock you down."

I put my arms around her and squeezed, her side burrowing into my chest as I pressed my forehead to her temple. "Just remember the girls and I are here to help you back up again if that happens."

She patted my hand and untangled herself from my hug. For all the flirtatiously outrageous things that came out of her mouth, she wasn't much of a hugger or even an affectionate person. She turned her face away, but not before I noticed the thinning of her lips.

"Are you okay?"

"Look." She pointed back out to the football pitch.

Drew's head bent toward Sierra's. He held a football in his hands. His fingers flexed then rewrapped around the leather.

"What is he doing?" My years of ignoring televised sports left me woefully ignorant.

"He's showing her how to place her fingers on the laces."

Grandma doilies and the tying of shoes entered my mind at the same time. I may not have been able to name a single person featured on ESPN, but even I knew Amanda hadn't meant either of those things.

"You know when you go on and on about glacier recession, thermal expansion, and salinity levels?"

"Yeah."

"Well, that what-in-the-world-is-she-talking-about feeling you're experiencing right now? That's how we all feel after one of your monologues."

So basically, in our group dynamics I was the essence of Ross and his dinosaurs from *Friends*. Great.

Amanda laughed at whatever expression my face pulled. "Don't worry about it. Just hold on a second."

She walked at a clipped rate and returned a minute later with a football, which she rotated until a row of white stitching faced up.

"These are the laces," she announced. Her fingers stretched as she gripped near the back pointy end, her pinky and ring finger on the laces while the side of her middle finger touched the last white stitch. "Quarterbacks—you know, the players who throw the ball after the snap—hold the ball like this in preparation to throw."

My stomach bottomed out. "Quarterback? You mean the guy everyone else is trying to knock to the ground?"

Amanda's brows drew down as my panic rose. "It's called a sack."

"I don't care if it's called fluffy bunnies. Why is he putting a target on my little girl? He can't make her quarterback. She'll get hurt!"

I registered pressure on my elbow but couldn't tear my gaze away from Sierra and Drew. She concentrated on whatever he was saying, then spread her feet and cocked the ball back.

Amanda shook my arm. "She's not going to get hurt, Nic."

I snorted. "That's right. Because no football player

has ever suffered from a concussion or been benched due to an injury." I could feel myself spiraling but couldn't get a grip on anything to stop myself from sliding further into panic. I knew in my head that I needed to give Sierra space to explore her interests and passions, but I also couldn't dislodge the mental image of her in the ER or being taken back for a CAT scan or an MRI.

She was my baby. My life. It was my job to protect her and keep her safe. How could I be doing that job well if I willingly allowed her to be put in a position that could cause her bodily harm?

"Nicole!" Amanda's sharp voice sliced through my snowballing thoughts. She placed her hands on either side of my face and forced me to meet her eyes. "First, breathe."

My chest expanded and nostrils flared as I consciously filled my lungs to capacity and slowly exhaled.

"Good." She pushed my face away from hers and back toward the practice happening fifty yards away. Sierra leaned back on her right leg, wound up her arm, then launched the ball in the air. The elongated spherical shape spiraled through the air, arcing then settling softly into a boy's arms.

My breath hitched. "Was that..." I didn't know sports, but there was something magical about the way the ball had gracefully sliced through the air and landed exactly where Sierra had meant to place it.

Amanda's cell phone appeared out of nowhere. "You mind?" She wiggled it a bit and pointed the top toward Sierra.

"No internet." My daughter didn't need to go viral for any reason.

Amanda already had the camera app open and recording. "Got it."

Again and again Drew would give some sort of direction to one of the boys. They'd run in a long, straight line or a short one, then all of a sudden change directions, but every time, Sierra would sail the ball across the expanse toward the intended target. Sometimes the catch would be made, other times not.

My heart swelled with pride, growing so large it hurt when Sierra jogged toward me, her face flushed from exertion and painted with joy. She sparked light, and my stomach rolled. I didn't want to douse the embers of her exuberance, but I also couldn't erase the memory of a guy from my high school football team being carted off the field on a stretcher.

Why couldn't she have been interested in something that didn't require so much...uh...contact? Calligraphy happened to be a beautiful and lost artform. Maybe the idea of raising kids in literal bubbles wasn't as bad as it sounded. You'd always know where they were, strangers had to keep their distance because of the physical boundaries around them, and the kids couldn't get hurt.

Wonder if I could get two-day shipping on one of those bad boys.

"Did you see me, Mom?" Sierra panted, her chest heaving from her quick sprint to me. "Did you see me throw the ball?"

I pushed a sweaty strand of caramel-colored hair away from her sticky forehead. "I saw. You were amazing." I grabbed a non-plastic reusable bottle of filtered water from my purse and handed it to her. Liquid leaked out of the side of her mouth as she chugged, dripping onto her shirt and darkening the material in spots.

"Think you'll be the first female quarterback to play for the NFL?"

My gaze cut to Amanda, my face morphing into a mom look. Narrowed eyes. Pinched face. I mentally screamed at her, *What do you think you're doing!?* and my furrowed brow added *young lady*.

She completely ignored my glare and grinned at Sierra.

"I don't know about that." Sierra's brown eyes, the ones she'd inherited from Greg, danced with excitement.

My fingers itched to curve around her arm and keep her close. To share with her the possibilities that lay ahead if she put on those expensive shoulder pads and helmet and let boys bigger than her slam her repeatedly into the ground.

"Stop being so dramatic about everything," Greg

had sneered when I'd voiced my concerns to him. If football had been my decision alone, Sierra probably wouldn't have been here.

And look at the happiness she'd miss out on, a voice in the back of my mind whispered.

I shook my head.

She wouldn't have been here. But decisions on how Sierra was raised weren't up to me alone. No matter that Greg didn't show up for Sierra as much as I'd like, he was still her father and (I guess) had the right to input on her upbringing.

With football, I'd simply been outnumbered. Funny how I was the only one actually with our daughter at her practice though.

"Coach Drew says I'm a natural. He called me his quarterback princess." Sierra slanted her big eyes my way. "But don't worry. I told him not to treat me any differently because of my gender. He looked at me funny, then laughed, so I told him I wasn't helpless and didn't need a dumb boy to rescue me. Then he said I wasn't that type of princess." Her lips scrunched to the side. "Who's Xena? He said I was a princess of her caliber."

Amanda choked on a laugh beside me.

My nerves were already wound tight with anxiety and helplessness. Fears real and imagined. They swirled in my middle, causing friction and heat. Drew might as well have added fuel to the trifecta. My gut burned.

I didn't need another male in my daughter's life exposing her to things—and, seriously, an overly sexualized TV character too scantily clad to ever realistically fight in a real war?—only to vanish, leaving me to pick up the pieces and explain things an eight-year-old shouldn't have to think and feel.

You're overreacting, that little voice whispered again.

But I was too worked up to rein in, and I stomped toward Drew. As if he was attuned to me, he turned. Our eyes locked, the horns of two butting rams.

Without dropping my gaze, he spoke over his shoulder. "Take over for a bit, Coach Eric."

The other coach watched my approach, frozen as if an impending natural disaster would soon hit. He spun and blew his whistle.

Drew stood his ground, his arms loose at his sides, his back slightly rounded. If there'd been something to lean on, he'd have lounged against it all relaxed and unaffected.

His body language reached out and twisted the knob on my internal thermometer. My skin flushed.

Did he take nothing seriously? Was everything just a big joke to him?

As if he could hear my inner thoughts, the corners of his lips twitched, then curved into a smirk. "What did I say or do to offend you this time?"

I halted in front of him, hands on my hips. "Are you implying I'm easily offended?"

His chin dipped, and he raked his gaze from the

tops of my red Tom slip-ons, past my planted palms, and up to my narrowed eyes. His brows rose, the smirk growing into a full grin.

I ground my molars together. "Maybe the problem isn't me. Maybe you're just really offensive. Did you ever think of that?"

Yes, I heard myself. I'd sunk to schoolyard tit-for-tats.

"Says the vegan who probably asks people to say tofu instead of cheese before she snaps their picture."

"Coming from the guy who probably watches reels on the internet of people crashing and hurting themselves and thinks it's funny."

His eyes lit. "One, those videos are hilarious. Two, reels are for cinema, not the internet."

"You knew what I meant."

"I probably know what you mean more than you think."

As if someone had taken blinders off me, I noticed how physically close we had become. Had we both unconsciously taken steps toward one another as we spoke? I stepped back, my legs a little unbalanced with annoyance.

Why had I walked over here in the first place?

Sierra's happy squeal reached me. Right.

"Don't play with my daughter's emotions, Drew." I spun on my heel and stalked away. But my retreat didn't prevent his quiet words from reaching me.

"Your daughter's, or yours?"

6
DREW

$\mathcal{M}$y body swayed over my feet, and I allowed my muscles to relax. My shoulder blades pressed against the wall first, followed by the back of my head, and then my eyelids slid shut, ghosted images of the fluorescent lights shifting against the blackness. A sigh exhaled from my chest.

Just a moment. One moment of stillness, then I'd push off the wall and continue down the corridor to the next patient.

But even in the stillness, my body felt in motion. The length of a stride. That slight back and forth. The swinging of hips.

Swinging of hips?

The dancing dots synchronized like a pendulum and the lighted silhouette my mind created resembled familiar curves, the shape transforming to the memory of Nicole walking away the day before.

Lazily, as if drunk on sleeplessness, the corners of my lips tipped.

No doubt Nicole saw her storming off after attempting to dress me down as a march of victory. Wonder what she'd think if she heard me say I'd wave a white flag just to watch her walk away again. As much as I enjoyed sparking the fire in her eyes and verbally crossing swords, there'd been something hypnotic about watching her retreating form.

Blood pumped through my veins like any other guy. I wasn't immune to a woman's figure, and Nicole's luscious contours awakened something in me that had lain dormant since Veronica.

"A dark supply closet works better for catching a few winks."

My elbows hit the wall to propel me forward, and I opened my eyes to the present. My best friend and colleague, Dr. Ben Reed, grinned at me.

He clapped a hand over my biceps. "You're dead on your feet. Dr. Stapleton wants you to head home. Take a shower, eat a nutritious meal, and go to bed."

I glanced at my wristwatch. "I will. I just have to do something first."

Ben gave me a knowing look. "Miranda?"

I let the Flynn Ryder smolder I used on the girls take over my face. "Can't let my lady think I've forgotten about her."

Ben shook his head with a laugh. "Heartbreaker."

My hands slid into the pockets of my scrubs. "What can I say?"

"Go on then." He shooed me away before swiping at the screen of a hospital-issued tablet.

I made a detour to the doctors' lounge and retrieved my old spruce Stradi violin. Miranda loved it when I serenaded her with bow and strings.

The elevator doors opened as I neared, and I stepped in before they slid back shut. An older woman stood in the far corner, eyeing me as I pressed the button for the third floor. Her gaze moved over my scrubs and down to the violin case in my hand. Her brows rose, curiosity nearly seeping from her pores.

I lifted the black case to cradle it across my chest. "The latest discovery in cutting edge medicine."

Those white bushels above her eyes folded, but the elevator slowed to a stop. The doors whooshed open, and I stepped out, bracing myself for the inevitable punch to the gut standing in this spot brought each time. The bright primary colors painted on the walls in geometric shapes were supposed to be cheery, but I'd never seen them that way. They'd been touched up in the seventeen years since I first laid my eyes on them, but the effect hadn't changed. Still mocking brightness in the face of a dark future.

I made my fingers unclench, the blood rushing back to my knuckles. Miranda didn't need me bringing my own baggage to her life. I came to make her laugh. See her beautiful smile. Help her forget, even for a moment, not wallow in my own memories.

I passed through double doors, nodded to the nurse at the nurses' station, and made my way to the community area.

Bright green eyes lit when they landed on me from across the room, and my heart tripped. Miranda deserved everything that was good and beautiful in this world. She made me a better man, and though I faced my own demons by coming here, she made me want to slay dragons for her.

She walked slowly across the room toward me. "You came," she said in a breathy voice.

That practiced smolder I'd given Ben returned. "Can't stay away from my girl."

She rolled her eyes and sounded like Rapunzel when she scolded, "Eugene."

I bowed at the waist. "Forgive me, your highness."

Her hand came up to hide a giggle, and I set the violin case on a table and unlatched the sides. "Would thou likest to hear a jaunty tune from your lowly and humble servant?"

She straightened her expression and pretended to arrange billowy skirts before taking a seat. With a bored look, she motioned for me to begin.

I quickly checked the tuning of the strings, making the small adjustments necessary, then with a couple of playful jumps to my brows, I let loose a toe-tapping tune.

"The Swallowtail Jig," an Irish fiddle song, leapt from the instrument like tiny leprechauns stomping out a Riverdance. The invisible pied pipers whirled through the room on each note, sprinkling fairy dust until the actual occupants of the space stood and tried to follow suit...or at least clap along to the beat.

Short bow strokes worked the muscles of my right shoulder while rapid finger placements of my left hand made the tendons in my wrist jump. It had been too long since I'd cradled the violin and made her sing with my touch.

I winked at Miranda, her face flushed with a rosy hue kissing her cheeks. A woman standing on the far wall caught my eye, and my gaze rose to meet hers as the melody changed to the next fiddle piece. Cupped hands covered the lower half of the woman's face, but tears brightened her eyes. She stared at me, then down at Miranda. My heart pinched, and I stumbled over the next note.

"Why do you keep going to the third floor?"

Ben had cornered me one day when we'd first started working at the hospital. He'd caught me sneaking down here, then witnessed what being here did to me. He couldn't understand why I'd continuously return to a place of pain.

I got his rationale. Understood why, after the sudden and devastating loss of his wife just hours after giving birth to their precious daughter, he refused to go anywhere near labor and delivery.

But Ben's black past and mine were different. He had the hope of a bright future and had found it in Molly. The darkness that had enveloped me here had farther reaching fingers—a span of a lifetime. And while the shadow of death had simply passed over L and D, it had come to reside at pediatric oncology. Hovering over innocents like Miranda. Six years old and battling neuroblastoma. Children her age should be playing tag around a playground, laughing and carefree. Not living around chemotherapy appointments and having favorite nurses instead of best friends.

I lifted the violin's bow for a moment of silence, then set it on the strings for the first strains of Miranda's favorite song: "I See the Light," from *Tangled*. I closed my eyes, imagining the darkness of this place being lit by thousands of lanterns. But a Disney princess couldn't vanquish this kind of void. Only a King could do that.

On the last note, I lowered the bow and violin to my sides, and with my eyes still closed, let my voice fill the silence.

"I lift my eyes up to the mountaintops
But where does my help comes from?
My help comes from the Lord
Creator of heaven and earth!

He will not let me fall
He'll catch me if I stumble.

Day and night, night and day
You watch over me
Lift me up and give me life.

I lift my eyes up to the mountaintops
But where does my help comes from?"

The old feelings of fear and pain and hopelessness washed over me then through me as a waterfall of peace, hope, and love rained down.

I opened my eyes and saw my fifteen-year-old self in the faces around me. Hair loss. Sunken cheeks. Open ports in their arms. IV stands by their sides like sentries. Chemotherapy leaving its fingerprint on their lives like an aggressive abuser.

The woman who'd been by the far corner had made her way closer. She stood now behind Miranda, her hand on my girl's shoulder.

No, not my girl. There'd never be a cherubic face with that title.

Unbidden, another young face materialized before my mind's eye. This one with rounded pink cheeks kissed by health. An arm that could throw a football with no limits but lived in unnecessary boundaries that confined instead of letting her shine. Where the children within these four walls were limited by barriers beyond their control, Sierra had no such limitations...

and yet her wings looked, at times, just as clipped and unable to soar.

My emotions were already a tangled mess. Frustration added itself to the knot in my chest.

I lowered to my haunches in front of Miranda and swallowed back the tears that threatened to spill over the dam I'd erected. Neither Miranda nor her mother needed more tears in their lives. Especially not from me.

I chucked a crooked finger under Miranda's chin. "You kick that cancer in the patootie, you hear me?"

She squared her thin shoulders, one side of her lips rising in a crooked grin. "I've been working on my roundhouse."

"That's my girl." I rose and caught Diane mouthing *Thank you.* I nodded, then replaced the violin in its case, waved at everyone, and hightailed it out of there.

Once outside, I doubled over, rested my palms on my knees, and gulped in fresh air.

Cancer sucked.

Even as a doctor, I felt it had the ability to tie my hands behind my back, making me as helpless to fight against the disease as I had been at fifteen. But I'd conquered it once and could only pray those kids back in the pediatric oncology unit did the same.

My feet dragged as I made my way to the staff parking lot, my legs as weighted as if I'd run a marathon. Exhaustion pulled at my body. Physically, from a sixteen-hour shift. Emotionally, from dueling violins with chemo.

I pulled out of the hospital exit and pointed the Suburban toward home. I'd gotten a text from Mom around ten last night saying she'd left an asparagus and tomato quiche in the refrigerator. I'd have wondered why she was out so late if I hadn't known she'd stopped at Ginny's beforehand with enough food to last a week. Sometimes living so close to family could bring drama, but that was a small price to pay for home-cooked meals just showing up in my refrigerator.

The traffic light changed to red, so I pushed my foot down on the brake pedal. The cross traffic passed through the intersection, and I covered a yawn with my hand. Music didn't work to keep me awake and alert, so I bypassed the radio dial and forced my gaze to read business signs and make intentional observations on my surroundings.

Café Laundré cleaners. Pushing Up Daisies floral shop. Love is in the Hair salon.

Wow. That small strip loved their kitschy-type names. From a marketing standpoint, probably made them easy to remember.

My gaze swept the cars in front of the strip and paused on an electric model. Not rare in Southern California, but the *Save the chubby unicorns* bumper sticker, complete with a picture of a white rhino, could only mean one thing.

Nicole.

Before my actions even registered, I flicked on my turn signal and made a right turn, pulling into the parking lot a moment later. I killed the engine and glanced at my reflection in the rearview mirror with a touch to the hair at my temples.

What a perfect time to get a trim.

*C*harlotte Bronson had some of the silkiest hair I'd ever run my fingers through. Long and fine. The stuff of shampoo commercials. But it was also unforgiving. Showing every scissor cut if a rooky took a blunt edge approach instead of feathering the tips. She'd grown her pixie out, so I'd exchanged the razor for a pair of shears.

"Should we go for some layers to add a bit of volume?" I asked, meeting her gaze in the mirror.

She tilted her chin, studying the lines of her tresses and how they fell around her face.

"You haven't steered me wrong in the past. If you think layers are a good idea, then let's try it."

I gave her a reassuring smile and traded the wide-toothed comb I'd used to untangle her wet hair for an all-purpose comb. The teeth glided through her locks.

A trim of the dead ends took no time at all. Next, the layers.

The sound of the entrance door opening stilled my hand. Felicity usually worked the reception desk, but she'd called in because of a stomach bug, leaving no one to greet incoming clients.

I craned my neck to see past the narrow partition separating individual work stations. Stacy was wrist deep in a color job and hair foils.

My hand slid down to Charlotte's shoulder. "I'll be right back."

"No worries."

I stepped back and pivoted on my heel, my face arranging itself into a friendly expression. "Welcome to Love is in the Hair. How can we—" The greeting died on my tongue. Not a natural death either, peacefully in its sleep; I murdered it in its tracks. Strangulation by gritted teeth. "What are you doing here?" I managed to choke out.

Drew's easy smile appeared heavier as he leaned against the reception counter. Dark circles curled under his eyes. Same as I'd seen on Ben's face after a long shift at the hospital. Horizontal lines ran along his forehead, giving weight to his normal care-free expression.

He ran his fingers through his hair, arresting my gaze. My traitorous eyes watched the motion, mesmerized by the way his hair bounced and rippled with his manipulation. I managed to tear my eyes away only to land on his knowing smirk.

Insufferable, full-of-himself man!

"I'm desperately in need of a cut." He emphasized the word desperate in a way that made my stomach impersonate Benedict Arnold.

Get ahold of yourself, Nicole. You're a woman of post-feminism. No one has control over your body but you. Certainly not an overgrown man-child.

My focus narrowed to around his ears. A number one guard would have to be used to get his hair any shorter. Although, the length on top flopped across his forehead in a casual manner, one that would be a crime for gel to try to confine.

"Yes, you obviously skipped a number of appointments at your barber," I replied drolly. "Unfortunately, all of our stylists are with clients at the moment." I eyed the door with meaning.

He straightened and turned, and my clenched muscles relaxed. Then he walked to one of the chairs and sat. He picked up a magazine and thumbed through it. "I'll wait."

My fingers curled around the shears in my hand. "It could be a while."

He looked up and locked eyes with me. "I'm an extremely patient man."

"More like extremely provoking," I muttered under my breath as I turned to head across the salon back to Charlotte.

"What was that?" Drew called after my retreating back.

I turned and smiled sweetly. "Someone will be with you as soon as possible."

I retrieved the comb I'd placed in my apron pocket and resumed my place behind Charlotte in the styling chair. "Sorry about that."

"I'm not." Her hand poked from under the black cape protecting her clothes from hair clippings and fanned her face. "Who's the man, if I may be so bold as to inquire?"

If I moved my gaze over a few inches, I could see Drew's relaxed form reflected in the mirror. I did *not* look over.

"Oh, he's my daughter's coach." And the best friend of the fiancé of one of *my* best friends. And the man who unwelcomingly barged his way into my life with annoying frequency. And the one who made me react irrationally all too often.

But best to keep those last few descriptors to myself.

"Really?" Charlotte seemed surprised, and her gaze didn't hesitate at all to slide over those few inches to study Drew.

I collected a section of hair from her crown and made a long, slow pull upward, sweeping the strands toward my face. "Yep." On an angle, I closed the shear's blades and the cutting edge did its job.

"You know he's into you, though, right?"

The hand with the comb paused over her head before descending back into her damp locks. "He just takes immense pleasure in annoying me."

"Exactly." Her eyes gleamed.

If annoying me equaled interest, then half the population must have a massive crush on me.

Charlotte snickered. "My husband is the same way, so trust me on this. He always says he only teases the people he likes, and he is unceasing in his teasing of me." She gave me a long-suffering look that didn't hide her secret delight. "Aren't I a lucky woman?"

Did boys not grow up to be men and leave behind the playground antics of pulling the braids of the girls they liked?

Greg had never been the type of guy to wink and flirt. When I'd met him, I'd thought to myself, *Finally, a man mature enough to not play games.* And I hadn't meant Monopoly. So many of my friends were getting hurt by the dating game. Greg had been refreshingly serious and straightforward. He'd never made my knees go weak or chased thoughts from my head, but I'd liked that about him. Not until later did I learn that wasn't who Greg was...just who he was with me.

Camille emerged from the breakroom, her arms raised and hands behind her head to adjust a bobby pin in her updo. "I'm back," she announced.

Stacy took a hair foil from the box. "We've got a walk in. He's waiting if you want to take care of him."

"Sure." She went and greeted Drew, leading him

back to her station, which just so happened to neighbor mine. As he passed behind me, the air shifted. A change in the atmosphere. What other reason would I have to lift my gaze? His eyes met mine and something within those ginger flecks put me on alert.

He stepped behind the divider, and a few seconds later the click of the metal snaps of the cape being secured at the back of his neck filled the void he'd left behind.

"Great weather we're having today, isn't it?" Camille's voice floated over the partition separating our spaces.

"Makes me glad I don't live up in Minnesota or Wisconsin. I saw on the news that they've already been hit with their first major snowstorm. So early, too."

Even if I hadn't known Drew sat just feet away, I'd have been able to recognize the voice as his. Somewhere between a baritone and a tenor, the timbre held a unique quality—deep, strong, and pleasant. A person didn't have to concentrate to hear the smile in his words. His good humor saturated every syllable.

"That sounds awful," Camille agreed.

Drew chuckled, the sound not quite sincere to my ears. "And the environmentalists want us to believe climate change is a real threat," he scoffed.

Camille gave a nervous chuckle, but didn't offer any form of rebuttal.

"I know some sources are calling it 'extreme weather'"—even with his disembodied voice, I could hear his air quotes—"but there's been extreme weather on this planet for as far back as there's been a record."

Was he serious? And could a person actually feel their blood pressure rising? Each vertebra in my spine locked in place, one after the other. And that "extreme weather" brewed in my gut, swirling like the beginning of a funnel cloud.

"I heard that Mars was warming, and it doesn't even have an atmosphere or people to produce greenhouse gasses to destroy it," Drew continued his monologue. "Also, that greenhouse gases aren't even the cause of climate change—if we even admit to such a thing—but that the increase in temperature is really a result of the sun, volcanoes, and other natural sources." He paused.

Around and around my middle spun.

"But seriously, the meteorologists can't even predict next week's weather. How in the world can they make future predictions accurately? And not that I believe everything scientists say, because they're only out for personal gain and those with any dissenting beliefs are being stifled, and, I mean, hello, Climategate scandal, but I read an article by a scientist the other day—"

Touchdown. I couldn't contain the force of the fury within me a minute longer. Two stomps to the side and I planted myself in Drew's line of sight through the mirror's reflection.

"First, over ninety-five percent of climate experts agree that humans are abusing this planet and causing climate change."

A slight twitch tugged at Drew's cheeks.

"Second, climate and weather are two different things. Cold temperatures and snowfall levels do not negate climate change."

His lips settled into a smirk.

"In fact, it's due to the dwindling sea ice that the polar vortex—which is supposed to stay at the north pole, by the way—has split in three places and states like Minnesota are feeling the record-breaking temperatures."

Drew's grin continued to spread. Why was he smiling like a fool during my verbal tongue-lashing? And his eyes shouldn't be twinkling like deuced shooting stars while receiving a clapback!

But his ginger irises kept dancing, as if tapping out a message in Morse code that said, "Got you!"

A joke. He'd deliberately said things he knew would set me off, for what? A reaction? And of course, I and my dramatic self played right into his hands.

All those words on my tongue jumbled into each other, tripping over their own feet in an ungraceful heap. If this was a dance, I didn't know the choreography.

"Oh, why don't you...you...grow up all ready!"

I didn't stay to witness his victorious expression, but Charlotte looked back at me with one of her own when I resumed my position behind her. She mouthed *He likes you* and winked.

I ignored her and finished adding the layers to her

hair. Picking up the blow dryer, I turned it on with relief. The noise of the motor would drown everyone out. Charlotte and her crazy notions, but especially Drew and his infuriating way of needling me.

Unfortunately, a blowout doesn't last forever. I returned the small appliance to the shelf and flicked the cape off Charlotte's front. "Voila."

She touched her hair. "Looks great. Thanks."

I followed her to the front and rang her up, then retrieved the broom to clean my station.

"Can I ask you something, Camille?" Drew's question taunted me to listen.

Say no. Say no.

"Sure."

I held back a groan.

"How do you help someone loosen up and have more fun?"

My grip tightened on the broom handle. *Don't let him bait you again.*

No matter what he said, I wouldn't respond this time. I'd stay in my own little corner and mind my own little business.

But that resolve didn't mean I couldn't argue with him in my mind.

Not that I'm trying to please a man, because I certainly am not, but if I were, it would be impossible. Too dramatic for Greg and too somber for Drew. Well, excuse me, Greg, for caring about things so deeply, and pardon me, Drew, for having responsibilities and not taking them lightly.

"That's an interesting question." The snip of shears punctuated Camille's reply.

"There's this person I know who I can't help but think would enjoy life more if she didn't take every little thing so seriously."

Well, life is a serious thing, Drew. We can't all skip-to-my-Lou-my-darling through it. Some of us have to be actual adults.

"And maybe I shouldn't let it bother me..." Drew continued.

No, you absolutely shouldn't. I'm not your concern.

"...but she has a daughter. And while the daughter hasn't lost all ability to enjoy life, I've noticed her mimicking her mother's somber mien, and I just think kids should be kids. Have fun. Enjoy childhood. Be innocent as long as possible. The world rips that away all too quickly as it is."

"Have you talked with her about any of this?" Camille asked.

My head rose from the pile of hair I'd collected, and my eyes snapped to Drew's. "He just did."

8

DREW

"Nicole." I grabbed a fistful of black material and yanked, the snaps holding the cape closed at the back of my neck protesting with a *pop!* My feet tangled on the footrest of the chair. Blast! She'd make it out the door before I could even stand up. "Nicole, wait!"

Her backside offered a nice view, but this time I couldn't just watch her storm away. I had to chase after her. Offer an apology.

Stopping at the salon had been a bad idea. Visiting a piece of my personal history in the oncology unit, seeing all the kids currently fighting for their lives, left me in a weird headspace. Not to mention the long hours from my shift. I should have gone home and gotten some sleep.

But I'd seen her car, and something inside clicked to

autopilot. And apparently stayed that way until I'd not just toed a line but jumped so far over it that I'd have to crawl back on my hands and knees.

The front door opened with a rattle—of course she wouldn't wait—and I dug into the deep pocket of my scrubs and withdrew my wallet. I pulled out a fifty-dollar bill and laid it on the counter without a backward glance.

The sun blinded me when I stepped outside, and I blinked against its harsh affront. Shielding my eyes, I looked left and right, then spotted her rounding the corner to the other side of the building. I jogged to catch up, then slowed my pace to match hers.

"For someone who isn't afraid to throw some verbal punches, you sure do run away a lot after you get your jab in." I threw a small smile her way, hoping my attempt at humor and charm would dial down her degrees of anger. I needed her to at least hear me out, and she couldn't do that with steam coming out of her ears.

"Keeps me out of prison on murder charges," she said through clenched teeth.

I reached out and took ahold of her wrist, gently pulling her to a stop. She turned, yanked her hand away, and squared off. Feet braced, she pushed her shoulders back.

"What, Drew?" Hurt thickened her voice. "What else could you possibly have to say that you didn't already say back there?"

I swallowed down regret, wishing I could go back and stop myself from trying to get a rise out of her over climate change. I'd let Miranda and the other kids fighting cancer take up residence in my mind. Disease had stolen their childhood. Fun looked and sounded different for a lot of them. And it wasn't fair. Sierra didn't have those roadblocks. Her life should be filled with giggles and shenanigans and carefree splendor.

I met her gaze, hoping she saw my sincerity. "I'm sorry."

She scoffed and looked away, but not before I could see her pushing down emotions of her own. Even so, she stayed standing in front of me.

"I shouldn't have said anything about you or Sierra. It's just—"

Her tongue clicked as she shook her head, a derisive laugh cutting me off. "Why do people do that? Offer a semblance of an apology only to follow it up with a 'but' or 'just.' 'But' and 'just' only negate everything you've said previously. Apologies don't need to be given with a side of justification."

Control slowly slipped through my fingers. Yeah, I'd been wrong to voice my insinuation that Sierra didn't have enough fun and that the too-serious apple didn't fall far from the strait-laced tree. Wasn't my place to speak up. However, I hadn't been wrong, either.

"I don't know." I laid the sarcasm on like thick frosting. "Maybe the same reason why people shut others down and aren't willing to listen to another perspective or where someone else is coming from."

Her blue eyes flashed, lightning over a cloudless sky. "Are you calling me close-minded?"

I forced myself to lounge against the exterior wall. The swirls of stucco bit into the back of my arm. I propped the sole of one foot against the hard surface, hoping I looked like I couldn't care less. I wanted—no, *needed*—to care less. After all, what was it to me if Nicole and Sierra didn't smile or laugh nearly often enough?

"Yes. As well as being sanctimonious."

The pulse point in her neck thrummed, her voice going eerily quiet. "When you have kids of your own someday, you can make all the decisions. Until then—"

"I can't." I cut her off, surprising both of us. Why had I said that? The last person I'd uttered those words to had eventually left me cradling an unwanted ring in my palm.

But maybe that was why. Maybe I wanted to see if she'd walk away one final time.

Or if she'd stay.

"What?" Her breath fanned over me, and I realized again our heated words had worked like two opposite-charged ions, attracting and pulling us toward the other.

I moistened my dry lips and looked over Nicole's shoulder. People expected women to dream of being mothers one day. To envision their life with a sound-track of pitter-pattering feet, kissing booboos, and waking up on Christmas morning with the wonderment and joy only a child can bring.

For a doctor to sit down with a man and give him the news that he's infertile—that those trusting eyes would never look up to him and call him daddy, that there would never be monsters to chase from closets or tea parties with teddy bears? Well, that wasn't supposed to be as devastating as it would be for a woman.

And yet I'd forever exist with a hole in my heart.

I cleared my throat, hating the show of emotion. "I can't have kids."

Her head tilted. If her temper had worked like a steam engine (which it wouldn't, because coal wasn't a renewable resource, and this was Nicole), then the tiny guy shoveling the black diamond into her furnace would have just slowed, dropping her temperature.

"Of course not now. But when you marry. Someday."

I shook my head. "Not someday. Not ever."

Confusion swirled in her eyes.

Best to get it over with. "When I was fifteen, I was diagnosed with testicular cancer."

Her breath sucked through her teeth.

"I underwent surgery and chemotherapy."

"I'm so sorry," Nicole whispered.

"Lasting effects differ with patients, but after treatment, after the fear of the cancer spreading subsided, the doctor gave me the news. Chemotherapy had made me sterile. They'd hoped that after a few years...but nothing has changed. I won't ever be able to father children."

She reached out and lightly touched my arm for the length of a heartbeat, then lowered her hand. "I don't want to sound blasé, but there are other options. Adoption, for one."

She kept talking, saying something about how many fatherless children there were in the world. A ringing in my ears cut her off, like the audio feedback of a microphone.

"I thought we'd agreed to adopt?" My voice sounded hollow as I stared at the engagement ring lying in my palm. The same ring that had graced Veronica's finger just minutes before.

Her eyes shone with tears, one escaping to run down her cheek. "I thought I'd be happy with adoption, but I realize now I was just fooling myself. I want to carry a baby in my womb, Drew. My baby." She pressed her palms to her belly. "I want to feel the tiny kicks and hear its heartbeat at the doctor's office. I want sonograms and morning sickness and the whole experience of bringing a life into the world." Her voice broke. "I thought adoption would be enough, but I know now it's not."

And *I* hadn't been enough because I hadn't been able to give her those dreams.

I blinked back the memories, desperate to bring the present back into focus. Nicole stared at me, puzzlement in the crease between her brows.

I let my foot slide from the wall to the ground. "Anyway, I know you aren't interested in any of my explanations. *But*"—I emphasized the word and was rewarded with an uptick at the corner of her mouth —"before I decided I needed a haircut, that's where I'd been. At the same pediatric oncology unit I spent a lot of time at as a teenager. I go and visit the kids there now and then."

She absorbed my words before responding quietly. "And seeing those kids made you think of Sierra."

"I just think she could use a bit more fun in her life." I paused. Nicole had stopped yelling at me. Dare I add that she could stand to have more fun as well?

Her palms planted themselves on her hips, and a taunt entered her gaze. "Go ahead and say it. I know you think I'm boring."

I took a step closer to her, fully in her personal space now. Her head tilted up to maintain eye contact. I poured all my confused feelings into my look. "You're a lot of things, Nicole Applegate, but boring isn't one of them."

Her lips parted, but no sound carried past their lush softness.

Speechless? Nicole? My gaze flicked back to her eyes before falling again to her bow-like mouth.

Part of me was relieved we'd managed to finish a

conversation in each other's presence instead of one of us stalking off in a huff. The other part was disappointed her loss of words hadn't been because I'd kissed her silent.

Then again, there was always next time.

9

NICOLE

*T*he door opened on a squeaky hinge. *Really?* I sighed. Yet another thing to put on my mental to-do/responsibilities list. And Drew thought I didn't have enough fun. Little did he know spraying WD-40 on rusty metal was a blast. Right up there with snaking wet, gross hair out of the bathroom drains, cleaning up roach carcasses after spraying pesticides, and wrangling an ex-husband into spending more time with his daughter.

But yeah, loads of free time for *fun*.

"Sierra, I'm home," I called from the foyer as I hung the keys on a hook by the door and put my purse on the entry stand.

"We're in here," she yelled from the back of the house.

I walked down the short hall that opened to the dining room, kitchen to the right and living room to the left. Sierra sat at the head of the dining table, a giant poster board in front of her and an array of colorful markers strewn everywhere.

"What are you up to?" I asked as I bent to kiss the crown of her head.

My mom walked out of the kitchen holding a steaming mug in one hand and stirring the contents with the spoon in the other.

"Hi, Mama."

"Nicole," she sniffed.

O-o-okay. Still upset about the football thing. Good to know.

Sierra ran her hand over the glossy white rectangle of poster board. Along the bottom looked to be piles of trash. Some food containers and banana peels and a lot of plastic bottles. In the middle she'd drawn and colored the Earth. Bubble letters of different colors spelled out, *Don't trash the Earth. Reduce, Reuse, Recycle.*

Her head turned to look up at me, her brown eyes wide and young and innocent. Eagerness played across her face as she asked, "What do you think?"

I touched the corner of the poster. "This looks really good, Sierra." I gave her another kiss. "I'm so proud of you."

Sierra beamed as she stared back down at her creation.

Mama slid into a chair at the table. "I still say a well-worded letter sent to the principal, superintendent, and state officials will exact change more effectively than a simple poster hung in the cafeteria. Schools are among the largest waste generators in every city."

Sierra edged away from her grandmother so slightly I doubted Shirley would notice. But I did. I wrapped my hand around my daughter's shoulder and tucked her close to my side.

I injected a warning tone into my voice and chided my mother with a direct look. "Mama. It's wonderful, Sierra," I encouraged with a squeeze. "You did a great job."

Sierra picked up the markers closest to her and stuffed them back in the package. "And don't worry, Mom. I made sure to finish my homework first before I started working on the poster."

My sweet girl. From talking to some of the other moms of Sierra's classmates, I knew not every kid was as self-regulated as mine. But I never had to worry about hounding her on her schoolwork or chores. She'd always been a very responsible young lady.

"I just think she could use a bit more fun in her life. Kids should be kids and enjoy childhood."

Drew's voice popped the swelling pride in my chest like a sharp pin to the side of a balloon. There couldn't be any truth in his words, could there?

I pushed down the trepidation I felt at Sierra's possible answer but asked her anyway. "That's great. But...uh...have you done anything fun today?"

Her little brows pulled low over confused eyes.

Oh good gravy. Was having fun such a foreign

concept that the mere mention of the word befuddled my honors-student child?

"Making the poster was fun?" she asked instead of stated, as if there were a right or wrong answer to my pop quiz-type question and she wasn't sure if the one she'd given was correct.

I glanced at the poster again. A colorful display of artistry and creativity met my eye, and I took a fuller breath. Arts and crafts totally qualified as fun.

Drew was wrong. I wasn't robbing Sierra of her childhood. Just because we weren't as footloose and fancy free as he was didn't mean we didn't know how to enjoy life.

"Megan did invite me over to her house after school to play Minecraft, but I told her no because I know how you feel about video games."

Guilt nibbled at the foundation of my waning confidence until the matchsticks I'd built it on snapped under me and I was face first in a pile of my own made up garbage.

Maybe I *was* too tightly wound. Sure, I didn't think video games were the best use of a person's time, and I loved that my daughter wanted to make a difference in the world by advocating for a cleaner Earth, but friendships with other kids were important too.

"Did you want to go to Megan's and play Minecraft with her?"

That confused look overshadowed Sierra's face again. If she'd known about *The Twilight Zone*, she'd probably have suspected she was living an episode where body snatchers took over the screen. What kind of mother was I that my child couldn't comprehend a simple inquiry about her desire to play a game with a friend?

"I can call her mom and ask if you're still welcome, if you want to go," I offered with a feeble smile.

She blinked up at me. "Are you okay, Mom?"

"Yeah, Nicole. What's gotten into you?" The spoon in Mom's mug clinked on the rim.

Who might be the better question.

I forced my smile to brighten, which made Sierra edge away from me. My counterfeit cheeriness only served to freak her out. If I started grousing my opinions on any certain topic, she'd probably begin to relax.

Crime-a-nitally. Drew was right. Sierra was uncomfortable with the idea of fun but was perfectly content embroiled in a debate.

I needed to change. For Sierra. To model for her that it was okay to not live quite so rigidly. To bend ideals and compromise from time to time. But how? Mama had spoon-fed me impossible standards and expectations in the highchair, and my personality more than leaned toward passionate boldness. How could I be who Sierra needed me to be so she could still enjoy her childhood and grow up a well-rounded human being, while also staying true to who I was as a person?

The ringtone on my phone blared from my purse. Bless whoever was calling for saving me from my existential crisis. I dug past my wallet and Burt's Bees lip balm until my fingertips grazed the smooth surface of the cell's screen.

Greg's name lit up in color, and the beauty of a reprieve turned to ashes. Wishing I had the skin of a nine-banded armadillo, I tapped to accept the call. Greg's face whooshed onto the screen.

He hadn't changed much since the first time I ran into him in college. Some extra creases running the length of his forehead and a few lines fanning his eyes, but those were the only features that marched along with the drums of time. His hair still curled in thick waves instead of receding like I silently wished, and he hadn't added on a single potbelly pound.

The same couldn't be said for me. But women laid their bodies on the altar of sacrifice when they grew a tiny human in said bodies. Skin stretched. Organs shifted. Hips widened. Weight was gained—I ran my sweaty palm on the outside of my leg—and not easily lost.

Though, Chelsea from human resources and her perfect size-two body couldn't relate to stretch marks and a layer of flabby skin around the middle that just sort of flopped on the mattress when you lay on your side. She also probably didn't have to worry about peeing a little if she sneezed too hard.

Honestly, I wasn't sure if I disliked her more for those reasons or for stealing Greg.

Then again, no one could be stolen from a relationship if they didn't want to be someplace else in the first place. So, bladder control and clean underwear topped the dislike list.

"Hello, Nicole," Greg intoned.

"Hello, Greg." We'd agreed when we divorced that we would be civil. For Sierra's sake. Took all my self-control at times.

"May I speak to Sierra, please?"

I walked back down the hall. "Just a second."

Sierra placed the last marker back in the package, and I held out the phone to her. "It's your dad."

Her eyes brightened as she reached for the cell, holding the screen up to her face. "Hi, Dad."

"Hey, pumpkin."

It almost hurt—a true physical pain—to watch her talk to him. I loved seeing her light up. But the dimming and disappointment when he let her down was a knife to my heart. I could only hope this time would be different. That he'd show up or follow through with whatever promise fell too easily from his lips. Turning his back on me and our marriage was one thing, but he needed to work harder to maintain his relationship with his daughter.

"Guess what? Coach Drew said I throw the meanest spiral he's ever seen. He's going to have me play starting quarterback!" Sierra didn't squeal—she wasn't that type of girl—but she did radiate excitement.

"That's amazing. When's your first game?"

"You shouldn't eat those." Mama leaned her hip on

the counter, Sierra and Greg's conversation playing in the background.

I took a bite, the bitter and not-too-sweet chocolate substitute melting on my tongue. "Relax. It's ethically sourced carob. Not chocolate harvested by child slave labor on the Ivory Coast."

"I didn't mean that, although it's good to see I've raised a socially conscious daughter." She looked pointedly down to my size sixteen hips. "I mean *that*. A moment on your lips, forever on your..." She sashayed to prove her point.

Don't mind that I was vegan and put more fruits, veggies, and whole grains into my body than anyone else I knew, or that I stayed away from highly processed foods in general. Because of my pants size, I must have atrocious eating habits and be judged for a sweet indulgence. That wasn't even that sweet! It was carob for goodness' sake. Car-ob!

The conversation reminded me too much of the extra fries incident with David Brown. People needed to stop making assumptions and silent accusations about me and my body.

"I can't right now with this, Mama." I scooted around her and plopped myself into a dining chair. Not close enough to be in the camera frame of the phone, but close enough to listen in on the conversation. I needed to know of any promises Greg made so I could remind him and spare Sierra another disappointment.

"So you'll really be there this time? You promise?" Sierra gripped the phone in both hands.

Greg laughed like Sierra's repetition in asking was adorable and in no way a reflection of past experience. "I said I would, sweetheart. How could I miss my girl's debut? I can't wait to see you kick all the other kids' butts."

"Or learn about dedication and teamwork and sportsmanship," I muttered under my breath.

"Hey, kiddo, Chelsea needs me for something."

I glanced at the clock. Six whole minutes he managed to carve out for his daughter. Real Father of the Year material there.

"Oh." The shine in Sierra's eyes lost a bit of its sparkle. "But I wanted to talk to you about—"

"Next time, pumpkin. I gotta go. Love you."

"Love—" she started to say, but the connection had already been severed. "...you too." She handed me the phone and forced a smile.

I was her mom. I knew when she was faking cheeriness. Besides, I'd done the same thing minutes earlier.

"Dad says he'll be at my first game."

I reached over to hold her hand. "You'll have your own cheering section. Maybe I'll even get one of those big foam fingers and make up a chant about you being number one."

Her lips twitched but then flatlined again. Darn Greg. He only called about once a week. He should be able to spare more than six minutes.

"You know what we need?" I asked as I pushed off the table top.

"What?" Sierra stared up at me with a hint of interest.

"We need to have ourselves a little fun."

"What kind of fun?"

What kind, indeed. I searched my brain for things an eight-year-old would enjoy, but it was like walking into a dark room and not being able to find the light switch.

Sierra regarded me with hope. I couldn't let her down.

I may not have known off hand where to find fun.

But I knew someone who did.

10

DREW

"*Y*ou can't be serious." Nicole's gaze scanned the expansive property, taking in the bright colors and carnival-like amusements erected over every square inch of the place. Her mouth puckered, and a sort of queasy expression flitted across her face.

I laughed and pointed her toward the sign. "It's a family fun center, Nicole. Fun is literally in the name."

Her throat worked as she swallowed. "You're a doctor. You can't possibly think germy places like this are a good idea."

I stepped in front of her, blocking her view of the striped awning over the bumper boats pool and forcing her to look at me. With my fingertips, I gently pushed dimples into her cheeks, coercing her lips to spread.

She swatted my hands away.

"Smile. Fake it if you have to."

She grimaced instead.

"Fun always starts with a smile. Besides, you can trick your brain into happiness with the muscles of your face. The act of smiling produces a chemical reaction in your brain that releases happiness hormones. So even if you start with a fake smile, you'll eventually feel real happiness."

Her teeth bared in the worst imitation of a smile I'd ever seen. "I'm going to check your research."

I rocked back on my heels. "I would expect nothing less. But while you're looking stuff up, check out Proverbs 17:22. 'A cheerful heart is good medicine.'"

"'But a broken spirit saps a person's strength.' Yeah, okay, you've made your point."

"Are we going to stand here all day, or are we going to go in?"

My gaze shifted past Nicole to Betsy, one hand on a cocked hip, the other wrapped around Sierra's slim shoulders. Near her stood the rest of the sewing girls along with Ben and his daughter, Chloe. Funny that I hadn't noticed any of them pull up or get out of their cars.

One of Nicole's brows rose. "I didn't realize this had become a group event."

Molly bent down and let Chloe climb up on her back for a piggyback ride. "My fault. Ben found out about your plans and mentioned them to me, and I thought it sounded like a nice break from wedding planning and mentioned the outing to Jocelyn."

"And I wasn't about to miss seeing our Nicole here with a gun in her hands." Amanda tightened her ponytail.

"Gun?" Nicole squeaked.

I flashed Amanda a look, and Jocelyn leaned over and said the words marching through my brain. "Not helping."

"It's just laser tag," I said in an unaffected voice. Maybe some of my calm and nonchalance would rub off on Nicole. "It's not like you or Sierra will run off to join the NRA after a single game of laser tag."

"Mom?" Sierra's voice pulled Nicole's slightly dazed eyes around. Sierra looked unsure, as if maybe this whole thing had been a bad idea and they should just leave.

If I had to guess, I'd say it was that hesitancy that gave Nicole the strength to push her shoulders back and stare the fun house in the eye...er, front door.

"Let's do this," she said, like she was a marine about to infiltrate an enemy compound instead of a mom on a mission to show her daughter how to have a good time.

"You heard the woman." I swept my arm in a long arc, pointing at the entrance. "Move out."

"You're hilarious," Nicole deadpanned.

I grinned at her. "I'm glad to see you're beginning to notice my charms."

She scoffed, but a snicker bubbled out behind me. Looking over my shoulder, I locked eyes with Sierra and tossed her a co-conspirator wink. Amanda and Jocelyn exchanged knowing glances, but I pretended not to notice.

The scent of greasy pizza and birthday cake mingled in the air as soon as we entered. The pinging and music from the arcade games attacked our hearing as the neon lights and flashing bulbs assaulted our eyes. Stimuli for every sense.

"A unicorn!" Chloe squealed. "Daddy, look. They have a unicorn. Can I ride it?"

Sure enough, over in the corner was a small carousel-type, coin-operated, ride-on unicorn.

"We'll meet up with you guys after your laser tag game." Ben scooped Chloe off Molly's back, causing the four-year-old to squeal again, and settled her on his shoulders before galloping across the room to the horned pony.

"Have fun." Molly hip-checked Nicole, then followed after her fiancé and his daughter.

"Okay, so how should we divide up the teams?" Amanda asked.

"Sierra should be a team captain," Jocelyn said.

Ringing from an arcade game rent the air, and we all paused until it stopped.

"I want Mr. Drew on my team." Sierra pointed at me.

Nicole gaped in mock horror at her daughter. "You're choosing him over your own mother? I gave you life!"

Sierra giggled. "Sorry, Mom, but I kind of want to win."

Everyone laughed, and Nicole shrugged. "That's fair, I guess."

I nudged Sierra with my elbow. "Who else do you want on your team?"

Her gaze roamed past Nicole and Jocelyn and vacillated between Amanda and Betsy. Under her breath I caught her whispering *Eeny, meeny, miny, mo.*

"I choose Amanda," she finally declared.

Betsy bent at the waist and stared Sierra in the eye. "You're going down, squirt."

Sierra taunted, "You can't shoot what you can't catch."

My gaze unconsciously found Nicole's, and I was surprised to see she was looking back at me. A sharp pain stabbed between my ribs.

She's not your kid. You don't get to look at her mom with a silent did-you-just-hear-what-our-kid-said look in your eye.

You'll never get to share that look with someone.

My gaze fell to the floor, and I mentally kicked myself.

I'd learned with Veronica that some doors would remain shut to me forever. And it wasn't like Nicole and I were a couple. She could barely stand me and had only called because she thought I was an immature creature who could get her daughter to laugh more. But that didn't get me access to secret looks or a deeper connection to her or her daughter than she was willing to give.

The desk worker took our money and handed us vests with light up squares on the shoulders and chest, along with laser guns for each of us. We listened to the instructions and rules, then the attendant finally opened the doors and let us in.

I held my gun across my chest, bending my knees and crab-walking sideways. I swung dramatically left and right and was rewarded with another giggle from Sierra.

Black lights overhead made her white shirt glow, but the best part had to be her teeth shining behind a smile like a seventy-five watt bulb.

I bent to pretend whisper in her ear, having to keep my voice at a regular volume to be heard over the mood-setting music putting down a steady beat. "What's the game plan, Captain?"

Sierra had always struck me as a serious kid. She turned her no-nonsense eyes to me that didn't even hint at flippancy and said, "Win."

I gave her a mock salute and pressed my back against one of the cushioned columns in the room to take cover. Sierra followed my example.

"Watch my six," Amanda said as she stalked forward.

Sierra and I peeked out from opposite sides of the column to see.

The red square of the other team's vest lit from

around a barricade on the left side. "There." I motioned to Sierra. "Do you see Jocelyn at the ten o'clock position?"

"I see her." Sierra's voice floated over to me from the other side of the column.

"Think you can make the shot?"

"I'll try." She sounded determined.

A beam of light, and Jocelyn's vest flashed.

"You got her." Unnatural pride thickened my voice. "Now she'll have to go back to her base to revive."

Amanda's vest flashed, and she turned and staggered back to us, clutching her chest and reaching out with Hollywood flair. "I'm hit," she croaked. "Save yourselves. Avenge my name." She fell to her knees then twisted to lie on her back on the floor, pretending to die.

"Stop messing around." Sierra sounded like Nicole. "Revive and get back in the game. I'm going to see if I can hit one of the targets to get us more points."

"They don't call kids mini-mes for nothing." Amanda stood and walked back to where our team's base was located.

Sierra went to the edge and started forward. I followed behind her on the opposite side of the room, watching for glowing forms and moving targets under the black light.

The point of the game was to accumulate as many points as possible individually and as a team by shooting targets placed around the game area as well as eliminating your opponents.

The game had a different objective for me this time, however. Namely, the Applegate ladies.

And I couldn't wait to ferret out Nicole.

Some *pew pew* sounds came from my right, reminding me of the fight scenes from space opera movies. Sierra laughed, and I imagined she'd found one of the extra point targets.

"Well, well, well. Who do we have here?"

Nicole's voice had me whipping my head back around. She'd gotten the drop on me. I had my laser in both hands, finger on the trigger, but hers was already aimed straight at me.

"Careful, Nicole. You're starting to look comfortable with a weapon in your hand. Today a laser, tomorrow an AK-47."

The laser bounced in her hand, but she righted it.

"You're doing it again," she accused.

"Doing what?" I asked innocently, although I knew exactly what she was talking about.

"Trying to get in my head and mess with me. Stop it."

My lips curled. "Now, why would I do something like that?"

The end of the laser moved slightly to the left. "I don't know *why* you mess with me."

Because it's fun. "No, I mean why would I stop?" I

smiled wide, knowing the black light on my teeth was a beacon. Then again, I already had a bead drawn on me.

"Because I could shoot you." She readjusted her grip.

"I'm not sure you have it in you to pull that trigger," I taunted. If I pushed her far enough, she'd let go and squeeze. Whatever fear or restriction held her back would be overcome, and maybe she'd see that laser tag and other such fun things weren't gateways to self-armament or whatever crazed path she thought they led to.

She moved her hands on the laser, and for the first time I noticed the awkward and unnatural way she held it. Like she'd never even had a toy gun in her hands before.

"Let me guess. Your mom didn't let you play with toy weapons? No NERF guns or Super Soakers growing up?"

A bead of sweat rolled down her temple. "How'd you know?"

The tight knot that was the Applegate ladies wouldn't be unwound in one game of laser tag or even a whole day at a family fun center, no matter how many rounds of putt-putt golf, how many laps around the go-kart track, or how many balls hit in the batting cages.

But the unyielding tangle of loops *could* loosen.

I lifted my laser gun and aimed it at Nicole. "Time's

up, sweetheart. You have three seconds to shoot me, or I'm going to pull this here trigger."

Her eyes widened, and she sucked in a breath.

"One...two..."

Come on, Nicole. You can do it.

"Three." I waited half a second longer.

Nicole's eyes squeezed shut, and the lights on my vest flashed.

There wasn't a bang because these weren't real guns, but I felt something hard slam into my chest anyway. But instead of being painful, the opposite was true. The moment had knocked my breath away and left me with a feeling of lightness. I hoped Nicole felt it too.

Her eyes opened, and a breathy laugh slipped past her lips.

"How do you feel?" I asked, then winced at the eagerness I heard in my tone.

"I feel...I feel..." Her smile glowed. Literally. "I feel empowered. And like I want to shoot something else."

I chuckled. "There are some targets over there, G.I. Jane." I took a couple of steps backward. "Just know that was the only free shot I'm going to let you have. I'm coming for you now, Nicole."

Maybe in more ways than one.

11

NICOLE

*N*ote to self: never play laser tag again.

Coming out of the dark room with its glowing surfaces had been like waking up after sleeping late on a Saturday morning to find the sun shining through my window and hitting me square in the face. I had to blink a few times to reorient myself as to where I was.

And slow my racing heart.

Adrenaline coursed through my body like a drag racer, dangerous and illegal. Or at least, it should've been illegal. No wonder some people became adrenaline junkies. The euphoric high was super addictive. And like a conscientious person, I stayed away from addictive substances.

Another mole popped his head through a hole, and I wacked the plastic rodent with the mallet. Lights flashed, and tickets spewed from the machine.

After this. I'd stay away after this.

"Wow. You have hidden talents, Nicole." Molly sidled up to me and fingered the loops of tickets I'd placed on the corner of the machine while I played.

I ripped the perforated edge of the stream of tickets I'd just won. "Beginner's luck."

Ben, never too far away from Molly when they were together, came to stand on the other side of his fiancée, Chloe in his arms, clutching a stuffed monkey he'd managed to finally win in the claw machine. Would have been cheaper just to buy the stuffy at a store rather than keep slipping coins in that machine.

"Don't tell me you've never been to an arcade before," he said.

I looped my tickets up and counted the tokens I had left over. Enough to play one more game. "If you met my mother, then you'd have no problem imagining such a thing."

He winced. "Pretty strict?"

"I guess. Although, she claimed higher standards. There were always more important things to do than games and such. And she's not wrong, you know. Why waste time seeking your own pleasures when you could be helping someone else?"

He nodded, considering. "I've always found it easier to pour out of myself to help others when I'm full first. Does that make sense?"

"Meaning you have to stop at a gas station and refill

your tank at times or you'll start running on fumes."
Jocelyn stepped out from behind a game.

I hadn't even seen her there.

Drew rounded another game set up in the middle of
the room. "Gas tanks? What are you talking about? She
drives an electric car."

Sierra jogged up, face flushed. "Mom, do you have
any tokens left?"

I gave her my last two, and she raced away with a
"Thanks" flying over her shoulder.

Okay, maybe I wouldn't stay away after all. Not if
places like this put that kind of shine in my kid's eyes.

"Guess I can count these now." I held up the tickets.

"Definitely have enough for a bouncy ball," Jocelyn
teased.

"A bouncy ball, a temporary princess tattoo, and a
lollipop," Molly said.

Chloe lifted her head off Ben's shoulder. "I want a
lollipop."

I counted off ten tickets and handed them to Chloe.
"There you go. That should be enough for a sucker."

"Yay," Ben said with zero enthusiasm. "More sugar."

Molly laughed. "By the time you get her home, she'll
have crashed from all the excitement of the day."

I kept reeling the loops of tickets through my
fingers.

"Way to go there, Applegate. With that many you
can get yourself the NERF gun and practice your aim."
Drew smirked.

Sierra joined our circle, her own tickets spilling over her hand. "Mom has a no gun rule for the house."

Drew cocked his brow in a way that looked like a challenge. "But she'll need the practice if she's going to beat us next time." He turned to Sierra and held up his hand for a high five.

"There are three hundred and ninety-two." I gave Sierra my tickets. "Choose your prize wisely."

Her eyes widened. "Thanks, Mom."

I followed her to the glass case that held bins of some of the smaller prizes, the larger ones hanging on the wall behind the employee exchanging tickets for prizes.

I felt a person behind me and somehow knew without a doubt that Drew had followed. How did I know it was him, though? Was it weird to be attuned to his presence? I could no longer claim to not stand the guy. Would even offer my thanks for this outing once I knew I could stomach the cocky, self-assured grin he'd respond with. But none of that explained this sort of sixth sense I had when he was around. This knowing of his location when we shared a space, even when I couldn't physically see him.

Like now.

The hairs on my arms stood on end as if an electrical charge pulsed through the air around me. Drew had taken a step closer. I could feel his body heat at my back.

My spine straightened, and I stood perfectly still.

"But Mommy, I really, really, really want the Elsa dress. Pleeease." A little girl about five years old stood with her mother at the glass case, her hand outstretched to the ice-blue costume hanging on the far wall.

"The dress is over seven hundred tickets, Penny. And you only have about two hundred." Her mom smoothed out her daughter's braid. "You can save what you have and get the dress when you earn enough."

"They go pretty quickly," the unhelpful employee stated.

Someone needed to teach the guy how *not* to incite a tantrum.

The little girl's lip quivered, and her mom sighed a tired sigh.

"Here," Sierra piped up. "You can have mine." She held out her cache of tickets.

The mom shook her head. "Oh, we couldn't possibly—"

But Sierra pushed the tickets to her and smiled at the girl. "You'll be the prettiest Elsa ever."

She blushed and tucked her chin. "Thank you."

Warm breath fanned across my cheek as Drew's lips brushed the tip of my ear. "You're a great mom. And you have an equally great kid there." He pulled away, and somehow I stumbled without even taking a step.

Sierra pivoted, a satisfied smile gracing her lips. I righted myself and pulled her to me in a side hug. "I'm proud of you."

She looked up at me. "I just did what you would do, Mom."

I wasn't completely failing. Relief lightened the weight of guilt I'd been feeling. Maybe my baby acted too serious and grown up for an eight-year-old, but she was also kind and caring. We could always work on the laughing more—like we did today.

"Now that we've all had our fun, are you guys ready to get some work done?" Jocelyn adjusted the strap of her off-the-shoulder blouse.

"How's the dress coming along?" Ben asked in a conspiratorial tone.

Molly gasped and swatted his arm. "You know the groom isn't allowed details of the wedding dress."

Ben pushed out his bottom lip, and we all saw where Chloe learned her pout. "Not even a hint?"

"Just know your bride will be beautiful." Jocelyn backed Molly up on keeping the dress details a surprise.

Ben got that love-sick goofy look on his face. "She always is."

Amanda awed, and Betsy made a gagging noise.

"You guys are going to sew after this?" Drew asked.

Jocelyn nodded. "We need to get some work done to finish on time for the wedding."

"Does Sierra want to come with me?"

What? That had come out of left field.

"I mean," Drew continued, "I was planning on going to my sister's and tossing the football with my nephew,

Owen. You know Owen, right Sierra? He's on the team."

"Yeah. Of course."

"Anyway, I thought if she wants, she can come along." He shoved his hands in the front pockets of his jeans.

"I don't know." My thoughts pulled in different directions. On the one hand, it would be nice for Sierra to have a positive male figure in her life. She had her dad, but Greg wasn't always stable and often left her disappointed. Although, who could say if Drew wouldn't do the same? And was it smart to let her get close to him?

"Please, Mom." Sierra copied the little girl's look when she'd stared longingly at the Elsa costume.

"Oh, all right."

Drew and Sierra high fived again, and I shook my head at their antics.

Fifteen minutes later, the girls and I gathered in Molly and Jocelyn's living room. Jocelyn had retreated to the kitchen, and the sound of the refrigerator opening and closing plus the tinkling of glasses hitting each other came from that direction.

Amanda let her head fall to the back of the couch. "Do you need help in there?" She shouted like a child instead of getting up and walking to the other room and asking the same question in a volume that wouldn't shatter everyone's eardrums.

Jocelyn emerged carrying a tray with champagne flutes and a chilled bottle of sparkling cider.

Molly perked from her position on the floor, her gaze honing in on the tall bottle. "Does that mean what I think it means?"

Jocelyn set the tray on the coffee table, then lifted her face to meet Molly's eyes. "Molly Jane Osbourne, it's time to try on your wedding dress for the very first time."

Molly clapped her hands, then jumped up to race around the table and squish Jocelyn in a tight hug.

"Careful. I'm going to need to breathe to make any alterations," Jocelyn teased.

Molly pulled away. "I'm just so happy." A telltale sheen appeared in her eyes, and she took a couple of rapid blinks. "I never thought...and you guys...it's just..."

"Okay, enough of that now," Betsy interrupted with a scowl. "Don't make me slap the hysterics out of you."

Molly laughed and took a deep breath. "I'm good now. No slapping required."

"I know you haven't picked out wedding shoes yet, but I need you to put on a pair of heels you think will be about the same height you'll end up choosing," Jocelyn said.

Molly chewed on her bottom lip.

"Dun, dun, dun," Amanda and Betsy chorused.

"What's with the face and the doom twins over

there?" Jocelyn straightened. "What aren't you telling me?"

"Ummm…" Molly hesitated. "I kind of already did buy a pair of shoes for the wedding." She ducked her head as if afraid of backlash from her announcement.

"Why am I getting a sick feeling in my stomach?" Jocelyn placed a hand at her middle.

I reached forward and opened the bottle of sparkling cider, pouring each flute about half full. "Cider?" I offered the first glass to Jocelyn to try and distract her.

"Can you go get the shoes, please?" Jocelyn asked in a controlled voice.

Molly left and came back, her shoulders hunched and gaze warry.

From my spot on the loveseat, I was able to get a peek at a pair of pristine white high-tops before Jocelyn was able to lay eyes on them.

"Jo Jo." Her nickname slipped out of my mouth. Thankfully, she looked over. I widened my eyes at her and gave her a small shake of my head. Hopefully she got the message. This was Molly's wedding. If she wanted to wear canvas shoes on her feet instead of a pair of bedazzled pumps, that was her choice.

Molly brought the chucks from behind her back, and Jocelyn sucked in a sharp breath. Her face contorted, but then she smoothed out her features.

"Keeping the simple…elegance." She stumbled over

the last word. "I may have to take the hem up a couple of inches, but at least we can get the fit just right."

Molly relaxed. "I know they aren't your style, but I want to be comfortable on my wedding day. Not afraid of tripping and doing a faceplant as I'm walking down the aisle."

"You sure you want to go with white, though?" Betsy picked up the glass I'd set on the table in front of her. "A leopard print would be cool. Or tie-dye." Her face remained the same as ever, and like so many times in the past, I wondered if she was joking or dead serious.

Jocelyn blanched. "I'm going to get the dress now." She hurried down the hall to her room.

"Are you nervous?" Amanda asked.

"To get married to Ben?" Molly placed her shoes on the floor. "No. When I think about joining my life with his, I only feel overwhelming happiness. Being nervous would mean I had doubts, wouldn't it? I've never had a single doubt that I wanted to be with Ben."

I looked down at my cider glass, glad Jocelyn had brought the drink out so I'd have something to do with my hands. Tiny bubbles clung to the sides, released and floated to the top, then popped.

I'd been a basket of nerves leading up to my wedding with Greg. Everyone assured me those feelings were natural. That lots of people experienced cold feet before the big day and not to worry about it.

I could never honestly say I wished I'd listened to

those confusing feelings or that I regretted marrying Greg. If I hadn't married him, then I wouldn't have Sierra, and I couldn't imagine my life without her. If I had the opportunity to go back and change my decisions or do it all over again, I'd repeat everything—even the pain and heartache. Because everything was worth it to have her.

Jocelyn reentered the living room carrying the dress form, her gorgeous creation of curves and fabric swathed over the mannequin-like figure.

Molly fanned her face, the waterworks threatening to start again. "It's so beautiful."

"Hurry up and try it on," Amanda demanded. "We're all waiting."

Jocelyn looked at Molly, the dress, then the rest of us. "I should have had you come back to the room to put the gown on instead of hauling it out here. Now I'll need to carry the dress back again."

"Don't worry about it." Molly stepped over to the windows and closed the blinds. "You guys know I'm not shy like that." She shimmied out of her pants, then pulled her shirt over her head.

Heat rushed to my cheeks as if I were the one disrobing in front of other people. If Molly had an online dating profile, words like *athletic* or *willowy* would be used to describe her physical form. She didn't seem at all uncomfortable stripping to her bra and undies in front of us. We were close—the best of friends—but paramedics would have to cut me out of my clothes before I'd reveal the rolls of my muffin top or the thunderous thickness of my thighs.

Jocelyn worked to free the dress from the form, then helped Molly into the gown.

"It's so soft." Molly ran her fingers over the textured satin fabric.

Jocelyn tugged on the short zipper in the back. "No bra on the wedding day. The boning and cups I've sewn in will give you enough support, and the back dips down too low to hide any bra straps." She made a few adjustments, then stood back. "There."

"Molly, you look stunning," Amanda said. "Ben's going to lose his mind when he sees you and want to skip the reception and head straight for the honeymoon."

Molly blushed but looked pleased.

"Jocelyn, you need to quit your budget analyst job." Betsy stood and walked closer to Molly, inspecting the dress and Jocelyn's design.

"Let's not get ahead of ourselves." Jocelyn waved her off.

Betsy snapped her head up. "I'm serious. I may be in music and not fashion, but I know talent when I see it, and you, girl, have got some serious mad skills. Don't waste them staring at spreadsheets all day."

It was Jocelyn's turn to blush. She coughed and refocused on Molly. "How does it feel?"

Molly glowed. "Like perfection."

"Hmm." Jocelyn ran her hand along the seams at the sides, her gaze as sharp as a detective's.

"There is one thing," Molly spoke up.

"What?" Jocelyn looked all over the dress to try and find the problem area.

"Can someone get me a mirror so I can see it too?"

We all laughed, and Betsy went to retrieve the full-length mirror from Molly's room. More exclamations followed, and Amanda had to hand Molly a tissue. Jocelyn threatened bodily harm if tears came anywhere near the fabric.

"All right, get busy. Those bridesmaids' dresses aren't going to make themselves." Jocelyn knelt in front of Molly, gathering the hem and pinning it in place.

I took out the dress I'd been working on and set up the sewing machine. Weddings inspired reflection in a lot of people besides the bride and groom. But the question knocking on my mind wasn't one I wanted to entertain: Would I ever want to remarry?

$\mathcal{F}$irst game of the season. It would be a coin toss to say who was more nervous, me or the kids.

I unwrapped another stick of gum and shoved it in my mouth, sending my jaw to work to expend some of the pent-up energy zooming through my body with nowhere to go.

Owen jogged across the field, the first player on the team to arrive. His smile stretched from endzone to endzone, shoulder pads to his chin and pads on his thighs making his legs look like they had some actual meat on their bones.

I held up my hand for a high five, and he slapped his palm against mine. "Ready?"

He pounded his chest with his helmet. "I'd like to see their rushers get past me."

I ruffled his hair, rubbing my knuckles across his skull. "That's what I like to hear."

There was something I'd been wondering, and I knew the kids probably wouldn't tell it to me straight, being an adult and the coach, but maybe they'd run their mouths when Eric and I weren't around.

I slung my arm across Owen's shoulders and drew him close. "Can I ask you something, man-to-man?"

His head tilted so he could look at me. "Sure, Uncle Drew."

"What do the other players think about Sierra? Are they going to give her a fair shake?"

He pushed his mouth to the side and glanced at the ground. "Some of them don't like having a girl on the team."

I'd figured as much. Not sure how I would have felt at their age either. Girls had been nothing but cootie carriers, and I had to make circles and dots on my arm for my cootie shot. But I'd also wanted to be on winning teams… "Even with her arm?"

Owen looked across the field where Eric unfolded a camping chair. Ginny slowly descended, one hand supporting her belly, until she finally sat. "Mom said Sierra makes the saying 'You throw like a girl' into a compliment."

"Yeah?"

He nodded. "She also said the best type of man is the one that can support a girl and let her shine."

My brows rose at the kid's flushed cheeks.

"I don't know why she said that," Owen mumbled.

"Something to file away for later." I leaned down to meet his eyes. "I'm going to let you in on another secret about being a man that some girls may not admit to."

He shifted on his feet. Obviously, he'd rather talk about football than girls, but sometimes a team sport lesson applied to another area of life.

"Now, some girls like to say they're independent and can take care of themselves." An image of Nicole, head high and proud, entered my mind. "And it's true; they are and they can. But just as a man needs to give a woman support to shine, he needs to protect her so no one else can blow out her light."

Owen fiddled with his mouth guard.

I clapped my hand on his shoulder pad. "What I'm trying to say is to play your position. Block all those rushers, and don't let anyone through. You're the line of defense for our quarterback princess."

My nephew's wide smile returned. "No one will get past me. Don't worry." He lifted his helmet to point. "Here come Will and Maddox."

Players from both teams trickled in. Families set up chairs along the sidelines to watch the game and cheer. Two refs in black-and-white stripes conversed near the middle of the field.

Sierra trotted over, fat black streaks under her eyes and twin braids dangling over her shoulder.

"How are you feeling?" I asked her.

In response, she held out her hand parallel to the

ground, fingers splayed. Not even a tremor. If I'd done the same thing, my hand's shaking could be charted on a Richter scale.

She didn't seem nervous at all. Must have gotten the ice in her veins from her mother. I'd never met another person so in control and sure of themselves. Admirable. And infuriating.

In a rare moment of uncertainty, Sierra chewed on her bottom lip and scanned the spectators bordering the sidelines. I spotted Nicole. She wore a pair of high-waisted jeans that hugged her curves and a checkered top that followed the natural lines of her upper body. She reminded me of a vintage pin-up girl come to life. Still modest but take-your-breath-away sexy. She had her sewing group friends with her minus Amanda, which struck me as odd since, out of all of them, she appreciated sports the most. But maybe she had a previous engagement. I'd heard wind that something big was going down at her job.

"Your mom is over there." I pointed Nicole out to Sierra.

I couldn't tell under all the pads, but I would have sworn her shoulders fell. "He said he'd be here. He promised."

"Who?"

There weren't any tears in her eyes when she looked up at me, but for some reason that punched me in the gut harder than if salty tracks had streaked over her cheeks.

"My dad."

So much packed in two small words. The hope in the heart of a daughter. The echo of defeat felt one too many times.

I wished I could say he'd be there. That he was just running late. But I couldn't be another male in her life lying to her. I turned her shoulders until she faced me. Bent so our eyes were on level, then drilled my gaze into hers so she'd know how serious I was. "His loss. Because he's about to miss the greatest game by the best youth QB I've ever seen."

Her lips twitched as if they wanted to smile.

My hands moved her to face her mom. "Look over there. What do you see?"

She shrugged. "It's my mom and Jocelyn, Molly, and Betsy."

"You have so many people here who love you and are cheering for you. Don't let them down, yeah?"

She looked at me, some of her spunk returning. "Yeah."

"Okay, then. Let's play some football."

The refs called the team captains to the center of the field, and Eric tapped Maddox on the helmet to run out for the coin toss. The kid had speed, stamina, and the stickiest fingers out of the bunch. He hadn't dropped a single ball in all our practices.

One ref tossed a coin in the air. A second later, he made a kicking motion by swinging his leg, then pointed to the other team. A smile broke past my thinly pressed lips. We received the ball first. Time to put some points on the board.

"Okay guys." I swung my gaze around to the kids huddled around me. Sierra's brown eyes watched me with intent. "And girl." I winked at her, and a few of the players looked her way and chuckled. "This is our first game, and I want you to go out there and have fun. Play your hardest, play fair and as a team, and have a good time. That's all I ask of you."

"And maybe make a few touchdowns," Sierra chimed in with a smirk.

I laughed. "Sure. Touchdowns are great, too."

"Don't worry, Coach." Will adjusted his pads. "Dad already gave me the 'Winning isn't everything' speech, like, a hundred times this morning. But I still want to try and beat the other team."

These kids had done for me what I was supposed to do for them. I went around tapping each of their helmets with an affectionate pat. "All right. Bring it in." I held out my hand, and a circle of smaller palms stacked on top. "On three, Panthers strong. One, two, three."

"Panthers strong!" we all yelled out.

I got Sierra's attention. "Double wing TE ninety pop pass backdoor." She nodded as the special team's players ran onto the field to receive the ball. Will caught it and ran for ten yards before getting tackled.

"You got this!" I shouted to the kids as offense

formed on the line of scrimmage. But I was back to convincing myself.

If I'd been a dad coach as all the other coaches seemed to be, then the unsettled feeling in the pit of my stomach would seem normal. But I had no personal stake in the outcome of the game. No kid of my own that would be affected by the events of the season.

My gaze landed on Sierra, the only girl on the field. I wiped my sweaty palms on the outside of my pants, a strange swell of pride pushing against the confines of my ribcage.

Probably a good thing I didn't know who her father was or where I could find him. I'd be tempted to leave Eric alone with coaching duties and drag the guy's sorry carcass back. Didn't he know the blessing he had in his daughter? What an amazing kid she was? Then again, his intellect could be called into question on multiple fronts. He had let Nicole slip through his fingers, after all.

The center lobbed the ball through his legs, and Sierra caught it, rotating the leather until her fingers lay on the laces like I'd shown her, all the while watching for the back tight end to get open. With a swing of her arm, she threw the ball, connecting with Maddox. He made it three steps before he was tackled. First play, first down.

A cheer broke out in our team's section of parents. I gave Sierra the next play and looked over to the crowd. Nicole had her cell phone to her ear, hand gesturing wildly as she paced back and forth like a caged animal. Looked like someone else had the same idea of giving the deadbeat a piece of their mind.

The first half of the game flew by. The ref blew his whistle, then tired, sweaty kids jogged over to the benches. Eric and I handed out waters, encouraging each player with a word or two. We'd made some good plays that resulted in two touchdowns, but so had the other team. We'd be going back into the second half with an even score, and I hoped that didn't discourage any of the players.

Like so many times over the past twenty-five minutes, I found myself glancing over to Nicole. She'd put her phone away and now stood talking with her friends. Her arms were crossed, and she seemed upset. Molly laid her hand on Nicole's shoulder. I wished I could sneak away for a minute. Nicole wouldn't appreciate me offering any sort of comfort. Especially not gathering her up in my arms in an attempt to shield her from the ugliness and pain in this world. But I could reignite that fire in her eyes. Nicole without a spark was like the ocean without waves.

"You like my mom, don't you?"

I startled and looked down to find Sierra at my side. She stared across the field at Nicole as well.

"It's okay if you do," she said. "I think she's pretty awesome, but she does seem to scare guys away." She peered up at me. "Are you scared of her?"

No point in hesitating. "Petrified."

She grinned then sobered. "Does that mean you're going to run away, too?"

I glanced back at Nicole. Her shoulders rose and fell as if she'd taken a huge sigh, then she shook her head at something Jocelyn had said.

My focus returned to Sierra. I should probably tell her that we shouldn't be discussing her mom like this. Goodness knew Nicole would be stark raving mad if she were aware. But Sierra looked up at me with her too-solemn expression. That grown-up eye-to-eye thing she did even though she was only eight. She was being dead serious and expected me to answer in kind.

If I were able to have kids, I'd want one just like Sierra. With her killer arm and fearlessness. Her compassion and old-soul eyes.

I knelt on the ground in front of her, aware this was a conversation better had off a sports field with a lot less spectators. "What do you want?"

She ran her hand over her braid in a self-conscious gesture. "I like you."

"I like you too."

She peeked at me from behind her lashes. "And my mom?"

I expelled a breath. "I like your mom too. But I don't think she likes me."

Sierra nodded vigorously. "Oh, she likes you."

"Did she say that?" I tugged at my ear.

She deflated a little. "No. But I know her. She's stubborn, but she likes you."

"So, I shouldn't take no for an answer then?"

Her eyes widened in horror. "You always take no for an answer. Especially if it's a girl telling you no. Didn't your mom teach you about boundaries and consent?"

I hid my laugh with a cough. "Yes, sorry. Not quite what I meant."

She gave me a look that held a pound of reprimand. "Mom is big on consent. Don't ever try to kiss her without seeking her permission first."

A strangled sound emitted from my throat. "Who said anything about kissing?"

She crossed her arms. "You don't want to kiss her?"

I glanced around, really hoping someone would save me from this conversation. Eric had the rest of the players huddled around him.

I swallowed hard. "I didn't say that." I mumbled my admittance. Truth was, I'd been wondering more and more what kissing Nicole would be like. Would her passionate spirit start a fire within me, causing me to burn from the inside out?

Sierra nodded once. "Then it's settled." She walked over to join her teammates.

My gaze found Nicole once more, and I traced the outline of her profile. If I asked for a kiss, I'd get slapped in the face. I shook my head. If only life were as uncomplicated as it was through the eyes of a child.

13

NICOLE

"*I*'m going to kill him." If there were a cartoon devil on my shoulder, he'd be laughing in glee at my declaration. But cartoon devils were always accompanied by cartoon angels and that little voice who whispered a reminder of the sixth commandment, "Thou shall not kill," followed by a quote from 1 John chiding that even hate for another person meant I'd committed murder in my heart.

I balled my hands into fists, relishing the bite of my nails in my palms. Sometimes supernatural beings of my imagination were a real buzzkill. Although, I knew the admonishment was true. After all, I was far from perfect and lived under God's grace. And I needed to extend that to others. Even Greg.

"We can have his body cremated and put into one of those living urns where his remains feed a tree," Betsy said in all seriousness. "Since he never contributed to society in life, he can finally give back in death,"

Jocelyn and Molly stared at her, slight horror written on their faces.

"How about we come up with a plan that doesn't land us all in jail for the rest of our lives," Jocelyn suggested, fluttering her delicate fingers in the air.

"Fine," Betsy huffed, as if she were put out by not being allowed to commit homicide.

"How do you think Sierra will take Greg not showing up?" Molly put a supportive hand on my shoulder.

I sighed and shook my head. "Unfortunately, this seems to be his MO. She'll be disappointed, but I think she's starting to not get her hopes up." My gaze found Sierra on the field. The ball snapped, and she caught it, then handed it to another kid to run down to the endzone, but he got pushed out of bounds a few yards from where they'd started.

"I pray that she isn't learning not to trust people. I don't want her growing up with so many walls around her heart that she won't let anyone in because her dad's a jerk who can't manage to be there for her when he says he will."

"Maybe she needs to see someone else let their guard down every once in a while." Jocelyn tilted her chin toward me, her direct eye contact a mixture of challenge and compassion.

If I'd had hackles, they'd have just risen. "What's that supposed to mean?"

"She means you're pricklier than a porcupine when it comes to men." Betsy rolled her eyes. "The species that can shoot their quills. You don't let guys get close enough to inject your barbs into them without the use of projectiles."

My mouth gaped before I snapped it shut. "That's rich, coming from you."

She shrugged like she couldn't care less. "Just calling it like I see it."

Molly's gaze darted frantically between Betsy and me. "Okay, maybe we all need to take a deep, cleansing breath before someone says something they regret. Words are like toothpaste, you know. Once they come out of the tube, you can't put them back in again."

A cheer erupted around us, parents clapping and whistling. I looked down the field to see Sierra and another kid receiving slaps on the back. The numbers on the scoreboard changed.

Shoot. I'd missed a touchdown by arguing with Betsy.

Sierra and some other players from her team ran to the sideline where Drew and Coach Eric stood, more kids spilling onto the field to replace the offensive line. Drew tapped the top of their helmets as they ran past. Sierra stopped in front of Drew. Her mouthguard and helmet couldn't hide the size of her wide smile. He gazed down at her, beaming.

My heart pinched. The scene was all wrong. Greg should be the proud father practically radiating love to Sierra. And Drew should be able to look at his own child the way he was looking at mine.

But if the scene was so wrong, then why did it feel completely right?

"So. Drew." Jocelyn's smile grew like the paper wrapper of a straw when Sierra crumpled it like an accordion then added a drop of water.

"What about Drew?"

Betsy huffed and folded her arms as if she was over my intentional cluelessness. Was she looking for a fight? I usually found her snark amusing, but if she wanted to go a few rounds, we could put on some gloves.

"Are you guys ever going to move past the foreplay stage?" Jocelyn's raised, perfectly sculpted eyebrows spoke as loud as her words.

"What?!" I thundered. They thought...that we... My mind blanked.

Molly's face turned bright pink. "Not physically. But you two have been verbally tangoing for months now."

"We have not been...tangoing." My stomach tightened. "I don't even like Drew."

Betsy barked a laugh. "Where's Maury Povich? We need him to say, 'The lie detector test determined that was a lie.'"

True. Somewhere along the way my dislike had

turned to grudging respect then to…something I couldn't identify. But one thing I did know. "He drives me crazy."

All three of my friends grinned at me.

"Exactly." Jocelyn smirked.

"You say that like it's a good thing."

"Oh, it's a very good thing." Molly attempted to waggle her eyebrows, but the movement made her face look as if she'd lost control of the muscles in her forehead.

Could my friends be right? Were Drew's and my interactions some kind of twisted non-physical foreplay?

Without any conscious thought, my gaze sought Drew out. Even though there were dozens of people, I was able to find him in seconds, like a pigeon instinctively knowing the direction of home. His broad shoulders filled out the team shirt he wore, but the ball cap on his head barely contained the thick waves of his hair. Brown ends snuck below the rim. My fingers itched to run through the strands, and a thin thread of jealousy snaked its way across my abdomen at the thought that Camille knew what his hair felt like and I didn't.

A female laugh shattered my perusal, widening my focus. How had I missed the trio of women creating a half circle around Drew? One of the women touched her neck, another reached out and touched Drew. He smiled at all of them, laughing at something one of them said.

My friends were wrong. Drew wasn't interested in me. How could he be when he had perfect specimens of the female form literally hanging all over him?

A bitter taste filled my mouth. Greg had left me for someone of more socially acceptable proportions. It had stung, but I'd brushed that part of our divorce off as his problem, not mine.

God didn't use a mold when He created men and women. Each of us were sculpted in His image, had love poured in and life granted. Every shape and size was a masterpiece of His creativity and boundless love. And because of that, I refused—or tried to anyway—to let myself feel smaller just because parts of me were bigger than some other women.

Even so, an ache settled against my breastbone. I threw my hand out to the foursome. "Drew wouldn't know a thing about a real relationship. He's too immature for something that takes true commitment."

I winced at my own words. They were harsh in my ears, and I wanted to take them back. But like Molly said, once the toothpaste squeezed out of the tube, you couldn't put it back in again.

Molly's face fell, Jocelyn shook her head, and Betsy just stared at me with her indelible expression that made me squirm.

"For someone who says she's open minded, you seem to have shut the door and passed judgement quickly in this case," Jocelyn said quietly, although I felt it as a shout in my chest.

"He was engaged once."

I turned to face Molly. Drew? Engaged?

"Ben told me."

"And guys say they don't gossip." Betsy spoke out of the side of her mouth.

Molly ignored her. "About a year ago, his fiancée called off the wedding."

Not my place. I shouldn't ask. But my tongue had other plans and formed the word, "Why?"

Molly looked uncertain. "Maybe you should ask him."

But the reason scratched at my brain and tore at my heart. Drew couldn't have kids. For some women, that would be a deal breaker. Poor Drew. Was he still heartbroken after being jilted? I wanted to march across the large patch of grass and shoo those three women away. Take Drew in my arms and give him a big hug. There were other ways of being a father than procreation. Fostering. Adopting. Becoming a stepfather.

I blinked long and slow at the formulation of that thought, the fragments floating around like dust particles in streaming sunlight. Before the thought could settle, Jocelyn emitted a high-pitched squeal. She sprinted as fast as her wedged heels allowed, then launched herself into a man's arms.

"Did we know Malachi was coming?" I asked.

Molly raised her hand in a waist-high shrug. "He

called about half an hour ago when he found the house empty. He wanted to surprise Jocelyn."

Malachi swung Jocelyn around before setting her back on firm ground and capturing her lips with his own.

"She seems to like surprises," Betsy said dryly.

The couple made their way back toward us, hand in hand. Color creeped into the tips of Malachi's ears as he met our knowing smirks.

He tipped his black cowboy hat at us. "Ladies."

"Malachi," we crooned in unison.

He pointed to the players lining back up on the line of scrimmage. "How's your girl doing?"

"The better question is, how is Nicole doing?" Jocelyn's laughing eyes found mine.

Malachi tugged Jocelyn in front of him, hooked his arms around her waist, and rested his chin on top of the silk headwrap tied artfully around her crown. "A bit different from chess, huh?"

Like a stroll in the park versus an alpine assent. Only one had given me heart attacks. When the other team had gotten past the guys who were blocking for Sierra, it had taken all my restraint not to go all mama bear on them. Especially when they'd slammed my baby girl into the ground. Only the fact that Sierra had bounced back up, and Drew was a doctor and seemed unconcerned, kept me from racing her to the emergency room to get checked out for a concussion.

My mom would have loved to preen about that.

"She's trouncing them about as well as she did you in chess," Betsy mocked.

Malachi's nose nuzzled Jocelyn's hair. Long distance relationship meant they made every second they were together count. "Good for her," he said. He suddenly lifted his head and looked around. "Where's Amanda?"

Jocelyn groaned. "Don't get them started on that again."

Betsy tugged on the hem of her *Speak to me at your own risk* T-shirt. "Seems like she's back to her old ways."

His mouth pulled into a frown. "What old ways are those?"

"She used to be a bit of a..." Molly searched for the right description.

"A flake," Betsy supplied.

Molly cringed. "We'd make plans, but she'd end up canceling all the time. She's been doing a lot better about not—"

"Flaking," Betsy interjected again.

Molly gave her the side eye. "Anyway, she was supposed to be here, but texted us at the last minute that something had come up."

"That's too bad." Malachi's gaze swung to the field. Instead of relaxing back into Jocelyn, he stood taller.

On alert, I found Sierra and fixated on her. "What is it?"

"I just saw the time clock. This is the last play to

score points. She's going to have to pass it long if they have any chance of winning the game."

Sierra pulled her arm back and let the ball fly, spiraling like a knife cutting through the air. My breath suspended. A kid in the same blue jersey as Sierra jumped up and pulled the ball out of the sky, landing in the end zone. The ref held up his arms, signaling a touchdown. The second ref blew his whistle to end the game. Our section of spectators erupted in cheers.

I stuck my thumb and forefinger in my mouth and blew a piercing whistle. Drew ran onto the field and lifted Sierra high before settling her on his shoulders, both of them pumping their fists into the air.

The wave of adrenaline I rode came crashing down, knocking the breath out of my lungs before pulling me back into depths I wasn't prepared for. Somehow, the filter I'd viewed Drew through had been peeled back from my eyes, and I was left wading through the confusion this new vision of him presented.

14

DREW

I replaced the stethoscope around my neck and offered the little girl on the exam table a reassuring smile before turning to her worried mother.

"The good news is that chest pain in children is usually caused by a benign or self-limited illness. There can be inflammation between the breastbone and ribs, or even a root cause of something like stress or anxiety."

Mrs. Turner nodded, listening closely to my every word.

"Just to rule out a few other things, I'm going to order a set of chest x-rays and an echocardiogram. I'll have a hospital attendant escort you to radiology then cardiology."

Her shoulders sagged in relief. "Thank you, Dr. Bauer."

I wagged my finger at Annabelle Turner. "You stop giving your mama a panic attack. She's supposed to have at least five more years of peace before you give her gray hairs."

The seven-year-old smiled, but her brows puckered in confusion.

My chair swiveled beneath me, and I peeled the nitrile exam gloves from my hands and tossed them in the trash by the door. "Okay, just wait here and the attendant will be by in a minute." I stepped out of the room and sent the order for the x-rays to radiology.

Ben sauntered up and leaned against the wall. "Lunch in the cafeteria?"

I glanced over at him. "Mom put a lasagna in my refrigerator yesterday, so I'll pass on whatever mystery meal the cafeteria is serving today."

"Where's your sense of adventure?"

"Not on speaking terms with my stomach."

Ben held up his hands in surrender. "All right. Grab your mama's-boy food and meet me in the courtyard in ten."

"Mama's boy? This from the guy who feasted on homemade dolmades yesterday while I suffered through a soggy tuna sandwich."

Ben just smiled. "Ten minutes."

"Yeah, I'll see you then."

Once I had someone lined up to show the Turners how to get to radiology, I grabbed the container of lasagna I'd stuffed in the refrigerator in the doctor's lounge and heated it in the microwave. I felt bad for the scent trail of garlic and onions I left wafting behind me, so I hurried to the stairwell and hoofed it down to the courtyard.

Manzanita trees grew around a cobblestone circle, offering shade to the trio of picnic tables. The landscaping department worked to keep the grounds looking nice for patients and families. Drought resistant plants such as aloe, yucca, and rosette succulents offered a variety of green shades. Fountain grass and wild lilacs had been interspersed for pops of color.

And I blamed my gardener mother for knowing and recognizing any of the plants here.

Half in the shade, half in the sun, I sat at the closest picnic table and removed the cover on the Tupperware. Spicy tomato mixed with Italian seasoning compelled my stomach to growl.

"I'll trade you."

I looked up expecting Ben but found Malachi setting a tray of food on the table, Ben a few paces behind.

"Hey, man. Good to see you." I stretched out my hand to shake his.

"Good enough to share half your lunch?" He removed his Stetson and placed it on the bench beside him. "When this guy"—he hooked his thumb at Ben —"invited me to eat with him, I didn't realize the food would be quite so…"

I peeked at his plate. "Mushy?"

Ben lowered to the side of the bench not occupied by a cowboy hat. "Unrecognizable?"

"Tasteless?"

Malachi unwrapped a roll of silverware. "You guys are really selling this meal."

Ben poked at his food. "Let's put it this way. We haven't died from eating here...yet."

"It's a good thing you didn't go into marketing," I teased.

We all bowed our heads and said a quick grace before picking up our eating utensils.

"How's the ranch?" I asked Malachi around a bite of noodles, ricotta, and vegetables.

He wiped his mouth with a napkin. "Really good. We've added more stock to the herd and have kept our reservation schedule fairly full."

"I'm looking forward to getting back out there for the wedding. It's nice to leave the bustle of the city every once in a while."

Malachi scooped a pile of potatoes that had more than likely been made from dehydrated flakes onto his fork. "I'm looking forward to that event being in the past. No offense," he directed at Ben.

"None taken." Ben lifted his bottle of Smart Water.

"My sister has become more than a little obsessed with the notion of adding the barn and property to a list of wedding venues. She seems to have forgotten that the Double B is a working ranch."

"Thanks for letting us have the wedding there." Ben

hitched his chin in Malachi's direction. "It means a lot to Molly and me."

Malachi looked down at his plate. "No problem."

"Speaking of Molly and the wedding..." Ben drilled his gaze across the table at me. "You know Molly considers her sewing club girls as her family. More sisters than just friends."

The weight of Ben's focus had my throat closing, and I swallowed down the bite I'd been chewing. He seemed to be waiting for a response from me, so I said, "Sure."

"And since I'm marrying Molly, that makes Jocelyn, Nicole, Betsy, and Amanda my family too. Sisters, if you will."

Malachi's neck twisted back and forth, regarding Ben then me. The quiet cowboy didn't say a word.

"So, as Nicole's unofficial brother, I have to ask."

"Please, don't," I muttered, seeing where this was heading.

"What are your intentions with Nicole?"

I groaned.

Malachi slid his tray over a foot and scooted down the bench.

Ben frowned at him. "What are you doing?"

"Getting out of the kill zone. When Nicole finds out you asked that question, she's going to be madder than a charging bull."

Doubt pressed furrowed lines into Ben's brow. "Well, it needs to be said." He turned back to me.

"You've been playing around with her for months now. Are you just passing the time amusing yourself, or are you going to get serious soon?"

I dropped my fork. "I don't see how Nicole or I are any of your business."

Ben's mouth firmed. "I consider you both friends, and I care about my friends. Especially if one of them plans to hurt the other."

The muscles in my back bunched, pulling my shoulder blades toward my spine. "I'm not planning on hurting Nicole."

"Maybe she's not the one I'm mostly worried about."

That didn't settle right. "You think she's going to hurt me?"

He balled up his napkin and tossed the paper product on his plate. "I think you're more invested in her than you tell yourself, and since you aren't being honest with yourself, you aren't being honest with her."

Malachi nodded in silent agreement.

I put the lid back on the Tupperware container. "You know, I liked it a lot better when we discussed the problems you two had with women."

Ben leaned forward. "So, you admit there's a problem"

I snagged his wadded napkin and threw it at him. "I won't deny there's an attraction to Nicole. At first, I couldn't decide if I wanted to shake her or kiss her."

"But now?" Malachi asked.

My lips curved up of their own accord as I imagined taking Nicole in my arms and putting her mouth to work on something other than a lecture...with her permission, of course.

"I think that says it all," Ben crowed.

Almost made me regret giving him a hard time about Molly when he'd dithered around with his feelings for his daughter's nanny. Almost, but not quite.

Malachi steepled his fingers. "Do you know how she feels about you?"

"I've moved up from abhorrent to tolerable, I think."

"That's...uh...something."

"Hey, Nicole's a passionate woman." Ben leaned back. "It may take less than you think to push her over the line from hate to love."

My grin felt a little evil. "Pushing Nicole has become one of my favorite pastimes."

Malachi lifted a finger. "Does pushing her buttons count?"

Ben shrugged while I nodded.

"But then we're back where I started with this conversation. Your intentions, Drew." Ben anchored his elbows to the picnic table top. "She's got a kid. When I started seriously considering a relationship with Molly, I had to think about Chloe more than my own feelings. Nicole's going to do the same."

Defenses rose within me. "I adore Sierra."

Ben's face softened. "I know you do. I'm just saying, that little girl has been through enough with her parents' divorce and her dad barely being present. You need to know—like, really be certain—that you're one-hundred percent serious about going the long-haul with Nicole before you take even the first step in that direction."

"It's not too late to turn back," Malachi added.

But the thousands of tiny protesters with picket signs in my brain all shouting *No!* told a different story. Nicole, with her activism and save-the-world mindset, had wheedled her way into my head and corrupted me. In the best possible way. Who knew if she'd ever actually save the planet, but right then I realized she could most definitely save me.

My lips tingled with the onslaught of a smile. I stood and picked up the empty food container. "Excuse me, gentlemen, but I seem to be in need of rescuing, and I know the perfect damsel for the job."

15

NICOLE

"Is that everything on the personal hygiene list?" I peered down into the shopping cart. Toothbrushes, toothpaste, deodorant, feminine products, soaps, and shampoos.

Sierra ran a finger down the slip of paper in her hand. "Yep."

"Where to next?"

Her finger paused. "The exciting world of socks and underwear."

I pushed the cart down the store aisle. "Live for a while without access to a washer and dryer and I bet you *would* find clean underwear and socks exciting."

Her nose scrunched as if her imagination conjured up the scent of unwashed clothes, let alone bodies.

We had a rotation of charities we shopped for each month. The battered women's shelter, the homeless shelter, the foster care advocate, and the children's hospital. These shopping sprees always left me feeling bittersweet. I sent up a prayer of thanks that I stood on this side of the exchange. That I had employment. A roof over my head, food in my belly, and wasn't a victim of violence. But empathy for those who would receive our paltry gifts caused a physical pain behind my breastbone. And, I wouldn't lie, a small measure of anger at my fellow humans for turning a blind eye to the suffering around them.

We stopped at the women's underwear section and added a few packages of various sizes to the buggy. Sierra pulled a package of Fruit of the Loom off the hook, and I touched the back of her hand. "Romans 12:13."

She didn't even hesitate. "When God's people are in need, be ready to help them." She let her package drop on top of the others. It balanced precariously before tumbling to rest beside a pile of deodorant. "Teresa of Avila."

I smiled and maneuvered to the adjacent section of men's undergarments. "'Christ has no body now but yours. No hand, no feet on earth but yours. Yours are the eyes through which he looks compassion in this world. Yours are the feet with which he walks to do good. Yours are the hands through which he blesses all the world.'"

This back and forth recitation of quotes had started on our first shopping trip. Sierra had spotted a brightly colored plush jaguar that reminded me of my own childhood of Lisa Frank notebooks, and she'd immediately asserted that she *had* to have it. As we'd been purchasing for the children's hospital, toys and plushies were on our list, but the conversation that ensued about thinking of others and how Jesus wanted us to show His love in a physical way by filling needs was a hard one for a preschooler to grasp.

We'd dropped our offerings at the hospital later that day, and while I'd been speaking to the coordinator, Sierra had slipped away to a small girl in a wheelchair. I still didn't know what the girls said to each other, but I'll never forget looking over and watching my daughter walk back to me, her coveted jaguar cradled in the other girl's arms and wide smiles on both their faces.

"That's probably enough socks, don't you think?" Our cart had little room left inside. "I saw a bin for five-dollar blankets. Let's grab a few of those and call it a day."

Unlike other kids, who'd go to the front of the buggy and stand on the metal part where the wheel attached to hitch a ride, Sierra walked uncomplaining beside me.

An endcap cut off my view of any shoppers coming in the intersecting direction. I paused, but when I didn't see the front of any carts, pushed my way forward.

Bump.

The collision vibrated through the metal, into my

hands, and up my arms. "I'm sorry!" I called out, only now seeing the corner of the other shopper's cart. I swung my buggy wide to clear the fender bender, another apology on my lips.

Eyes the color of ginger met mine. Surprise then amusement crinkled the corners and fanned out of those iridescent orbs. He leaned casually over the handle of his cart, his muscular forearms taking the brunt of his upper body weight.

"Mr. Drew!" Sierra bounced on the balls of her feet.

Drew's gaze slid from mine to Sierra's, and he bestowed one of his heart-stopping—yes, I was finally admitting the catch in my chest when he was near maybe wasn't completely due to annoyance—smiles on my daughter. "Hey, princess. How's my favorite quarterback?"

The bouncing turned to rocking on her heels. "Good."

Drew eyed the contents in the belly of our cart. "That's an interesting assortment you have there." His gaze rose and snagged mine.

"We're shopping for the homeless shelter," Sierra answered.

If possible, his face softened even more. "Why does that not surprise me?"

Sierra shrugged. "I don't know, but we were just about to get some blankets."

"Blankets you say?" He straightened. "What a coincidence. I need some blankets as well."

I shook my head at him. "You do not."

He turned his cart to face the same direction as mine. "How else am I supposed to stay warm at night?" He winked.

Heat crawled its way up my neck, and I looked away. It had been a long time since I'd kept anyone "warm" at night. Although I knew his innuendo was meant in jest, my core flamed.

In fight or flight situations, I usually chose option one. However, I found my feet beating a steady rhythm on the hard surface of the floor, a preservation instinct within me kicking in, creating distance between myself and Drew.

A part of me wished Drew had remained one dimensional. That in my mind at least, he'd stayed the flirtatious, immature man who liked to get his kicks at my expense and refused to grow up. *That* Drew could easily be filed away and dismissed.

But I'd spent too much time with him lately and seen more sides to him than I ever imagined he had. Now I was left with the question of what to do with this new version of Drew.

Without really paying attention to my actions, I grabbed a rolled-up fleece blanket and transferred it to the cart.

Drew pulled up beside me and picked up a blanket of his own. He tossed it between his hands then hiked it over his shoulder. "Sierra, go long."

"Don't even think about it," I warned them both, although my glare pinned on Drew.

He chuckled and tossed the blanket in his own buggy. "No, of course not."

Sierra fingered the fuzzy material and picked up a teal blanket.

"The floor is lava," Drew announced out of nowhere. "Five…four…"

Sierra's eyes grew wide, and she looked at me as if seeking permission.

"Three…"

My gaze swung to Drew, and he mouthed *fun*.

Right. Fun.

"Two…"

Oh, botheration. No harm in pretending the floor was lava for a second and picking up my feet so I wouldn't get fake burned. I put my back to the large metal bin placed in the middle of the wide aisle holding the blankets, set my palms on the top, and hoisted myself to perch on the rim.

Sierra jumped from her spot and landed on the front of the buggy like any other kid her age, while Drew took up the space beside me.

The problem with being a big bottomed girl, though, was that extra mass equaled more gravitational pull, and right then all that mass precariously shifted, my bottom sinking beneath me, folding my legs up to my chest.

I reached out, arms flapping to gain purchase on

something that would stop my descent and fall from grace. My fingers grazed fabric and reflexively curled, pulling.

But I kept falling, my balance now completely abandoning me. I squealed as my back hit the pile of blankets and sank beneath the surface into I-didn't-know-how-many layers. A second later, my sea of pillow-soft landing undulated, and a deep *oomph* emanated beside me.

I blinked, my canvas shoes outlined in front of the superstore's fluorescent lights. A groan I felt instead of heard rumbled against my ribs. I might as well have died of embarrassment, because slogging my body out of the plush coffin would be impossible.

The rolled blanket by my head moved. I looked over and sucked in a sharp breath. Drew's face lay only inches away. The intimacy of lying this closely beside him caused my pulse to thrum harder.

Hearts, as I'd always suspected, lacked any sense of logic. No matter our vicinity, we were two people who'd fallen into a store's display while playing a schoolyard game. No reason for racing pulses.

"Mrs. Applegate." Drew's spicy breath fanned over my face, the wisps of hair around my temple tickling my cheek with his every word. "I don't know what kind of man you think I am, but I don't go around letting women pull me under the covers with them."

And that grin, the one that had infuriated me

before, now caused my insides to shift, making me strangely...at ease.

Which, given our predicament, didn't make any sense at all.

Blankets around us moved, and I was thankful to be buried under fleece instead of rubble. A blanket near my face was taken away and revealed Sierra's huge grin.

"That was *so* funny."

Drew sat up, looked back at me, and offered me his hand. He had a firm and steady grip, but instead of releasing me when I once more sat in a vertical position, he squeezed.

A woman walked by, her eyes bugging at us in the display. Usually on the other end of those disapproving tsks, I squirmed and tucked my chin. I needed to get out of those blankets. Getting kicked out and banned from a store where some people didn't even bother throwing on a bra or changing from their pajamas to shop wasn't on my bucket list.

I shifted my weight, but the unstable cushion beneath me only rearranged to make more room, and I sank further. I gritted my teeth and hefted one leg forward. Blankets threatened to swallow me. All of my childhood fears of quicksand—I still suffered trauma from Artax and the Swamp of Sadness, thank you very much *Never Ending Story*—came back to me. Instead of sand, I'd eventually sink to the bottom of a pit of fleece.

Drew gripped the lip of the metal box-like thing

that currently jailed us and hauled his body over the side with the grace of a stag. Meanwhile, I managed to shuffle forward only to lose my balance again, flail my arms like windmills, and fall on my bum.

Drew chuckled.

I glared at him. "This was your bright idea. Are you going to help me out or just laugh at me?"

"Can't I do both?" His hands encased my wrists and pulled me forward.

I stood in front of him in my lake of fleece. "No."

He placed my hands behind his neck and let go of my wrists. A second later, his palms skidded across my hips, causing my stomach to dip to my toes. His gaze delved into mine, catching me off guard and probing deeper than I expected.

I was a zombie. Not in the eating brains sense but in the undead sense. Or was I both dead and alive? Or alive again? The state of zombies confused me...just like the swirl of desire that hit me low in my gut.

We probably only stood there seconds, but time had lost its grip on my reality. Unlike Drew's fingers that pressed into the swell of flesh that rounded over my hip bone.

"Are you ready?" he muttered, that invisible line connecting our gazes so taut that it reached into my core and anchored all the unsettled feelings there.

Ready for what? Somehow I knew his question meant more than a simple readiness to have my feet back on solid ground.

Not waiting for me to answer—and good thing, because we could have been there until the second coming otherwise—he hoisted me over the edge of the bin as if I weighed nothing, attempting to make a liar out of the scale.

My chest pressed against his, and like so many moments in the last few minutes, time slowed as if a Hollywood director had control over effects. My body slid down his front, friction creating unseen sparks at every point where our bodies touched.

By the time my feet hit the ground, my lungs were heaving oxygen like I'd attempted to climb Everest instead of simply being lifted a couple feet and returned to standing.

"Will you have dinner with me?" The confident, almost cocky expression he usually wore had been replaced with a hesitant vulnerability.

Sierra moved in my peripheral vision, finally snapping the cord tying me to Drew. I stepped away from him, and cleared my throat.

Drew glanced her way, a wry smile tugging at his lips. "What good are all the blankets without pillows? Would you mind grabbing some, princess?"

Her gaze bounced between us, her too-intelligent eyes sparkling. "Sure."

As soon as Sierra turned her back, Drew refocused on me. He held up a hand. "Before you turn me down flat, know that I am not above making a fool of myself in order for you to say yes. Although, please don't offer a bargain that involves money. Even in the name of charity. I get the willies just from those lunchbox auction things on shows like *Little House on the Prairie*. I'd feel like a perv if I had to pay in any way, shape, or form, to spend time with a woman. But if you want me to get on the store's intercom system right now and sing 'Can't Take My Eyes Off You' à la Heath Ledger to prove I'm serious, I'll do it."

A bubble of laughter worked its way up my chest. "How does acting a fool prove you're serious?"

"Oh, honey. If you have to ask, then you've never had someone woo you right."

I'd never had anyone woo me at all.

Sierra returned, hugging pillows to her middle like she planned to play Santa. Drew took a step closer, and I swore the hairs on my arm tried to reach out and touch him.

"I'll respect your answer if you say no, but I have to warn you, I can be stubborn, and I don't give up easy when I want something."

Everything stilled around me as I soaked in his meaning. Me. He wanted me. For the first time in probably ever, I found I didn't want to argue with Drew. "Pick me up at seven."

16

DREW

*A*t ten to seven, I knocked on Nicole's door. A handful of moths fluttered around the single bulb hanging from the porch light above my head. A siren wailed in the distance. My mouth flooded in a rare show of nerves, and I swallowed, mentally telling myself to calm down.

I hadn't been nervous about a date in a long time. But this was different. This was Nicole. While I'd casually dated since Veronica, I'd never been serious. Never had feelings for the woman other than wanting to spend the evening in someone's company instead of by myself. But there wasn't anything casual about my feelings for Nicole. She'd never said so, but being a mom raised the stakes. Like Ben said, she had more to consider than just herself.

Then again, so did I.

The door opened. Nicole stood in the frame, backlit

by the house lights. She had on a floral-patterned dress that nipped at the waist and pooled out like a bell, stopping at her knees. Where at the football game I'd thought she could be a vintage pin-up girl, her outfit tonight reminded me of a sweet and wholesome housewife from the 50s—some type of modern Donna Reed. Her hair had been rolled and pinned away from her face, a style I recognized from World War II movies.

"You look stunning."

She blushed and fiddled with the length of her dress. "Thank you."

"These are for you." I struck out my right hand and offered her a bouquet of warm-toned sunflowers.

Her fingers brushed mine as she wrapped them around the flowers' stems, and I moved my pinkie to caress the back of her hand as she pulled the bouquet to her.

She brought them to her face and inhaled. "These are lovely. Thank you."

Sierra popped her head out from behind Nicole's back. "Hi, Mr. Drew."

"Hey, princess." I held out the small bouquet of dahlias in my left hand. "These are for you."

Her eyes widened as she reached to accept my gift. "You brought me flowers?"

I winked at Nicole before wiping all vestiges of humor from my face and regarded Sierra as seriously as I could. "They pale in comparison to your beauty, but consider them a small token of my grandest affection, humbly bestowed by your most ardent admirer."

Sierra giggled, and Nicole rolled her eyes, a hint of a smile on her heart-shaped lips.

"Never trust a smooth talker, Sierra."

I grabbed at my chest. "I'm wounded by your implications and lack of faith in my sincerity."

Sierra giggled again.

Nicole placed a hand on her shoulder. "Be good for Grandma, okay?"

Sierra nodded, holding her flowers to her chest.

Nicole kissed her head. "Let me just grab my purse," she said to me.

When her back was turned, I leaned toward Sierra. "Be good, but maybe mix in a touch of mischief, eh?" I made my eyebrows jump and crossed my eyes while sticking out my tongue.

She leaned in closer to me as if to offer a secret of her own. "Maybe not so much mischief for you."

I tweaked her braid. "I can't make any promises."

Nicole walked back to the door. "What are you two whispering about?"

I straightened and put on a Shakespearean air. "You can torture me, madam, but I'll never tell."

I winked at Sierra. She tried to wink back, but her face mostly smooshed together. She reached a hand up and physically closed one eye.

Man, that kid was cute.

"Don't stay up too late." Nicole grabbed the door

handle and paused. "And only one show on TV." She worried her lip.

I watched the display, wondering if I should say something. Nicole seemed nervous to leave Sierra. Should I offer to grab take-out? We could do a picnic on the living room floor. I opened my mouth to offer at the same time as Sierra planted her free hand on Nicole's back and shoved.

"Go, Mom. I'll be fine. I'll even take care of Grandma."

Nicole stumbled over the threshold, and I reach out and steadied her with a hand to her elbow.

"Okay, smarty. No need to use force." Nicole faced the door, preparing for another last-minute instruction when Sierra slammed it in her face.

She turned to me, an apologetic, abashed look on her face. "Well, I guess that tells me how she feels about tonight's events."

I stuffed my hands in my front pockets to keep myself from reaching out to touch her. "And how do *you* feel?"

Her gaze dropped to the ground, and she clutched her purse handle in front of her. "I'm a little nervous, to be honest."

"Good."

Her head whipped up. "Good?"

I let a small smile unfurl. "I wouldn't want to be the only one with a case of the nerves."

Her shoulders relaxed, and she shook her head at me.

I hooked my elbow out toward her like a gentleman from another time. "Shall we?"

She placed her hand on my arm. "We shall."

I opened the passenger door of the Suburban for her. "Didn't I tell you the next time we went on a date I'd pick you up in my trusty steed? Bet you thought pigs would fly before that happened."

"You weren't serious then." She clicked in her seatbelt.

I waited until she met my gaze. "Wasn't I?"

Instead of waiting for her reply, I shut the door and rounded the hood.

It took about ten minutes to get to the restaurant, during which we bantered back and forth. When I pulled into the parking lot and killed the engine, I found Nicole staring at the industrial sign with hand-painted lettering.

"Is this okay?" I asked, beginning to feel I'd made some kind of mistake.

"You're taking me to Eden's?" There was a tone of something I couldn't identify in her voice.

"I checked the reviews and people seem to like the food, but if you'd rather go someplace else, we can."

"No, it's not that. It's just...you know this is a vegan restaurant, right?"

"Yeah," I said slowly. "And you're vegan."

As a doctor, I knew smiles couldn't literally stop

hearts, but as I watched Nicole's lips bloom into the prettiest picture, my cardiac rhythm skipped a beat.

Her head tilted, her hair falling over her shoulder. "Whenever I think I've got you figured out, you surprise me."

I twisted in the small space allotted between the seat and the steering wheel, giving her my full attention. "That means you haven't spent enough time with me." I gave her a look of teasing suggestion.

She shook her head and smiled. Two reactions I was becoming familiar with in response to my playfulness. "Then again, maybe you're exactly who I thought you were."

I reached out and touched a lock of her hair, letting its silk smooth across the pads of my fingertips as gravity pulled my hand down. "You're everything I didn't know I needed." My voice grew husky. My hand continued its downward descent, trailing her arm and landing at her open palm. I squeezed. "Come on. Let's get some food."

The restaurant sported a modern vibe, with a bank of floor-to-ceiling windows along one wall, exposed ductwork suspended from the ceiling, and greenery planted in sconces, hanging and cascading from thick boards with impressive wood grains against a red-brick wall. Dangling Edison bulbs over each table gave the dining room a warm glow.

The hostess greeted us as soon as we entered and showed us a table in the corner.

Nicole opened her menu. "I've never eaten here before." She peered up at me through her lashes. "You look surprised."

"That's because I am."

She shrugged. "Most guys prefer steak and potatoes to cauliflower and ancient grains."

"Go on a lot of dates, do you?"

A hidden smile played behind her flat lips. "Only when the Nature Conservancy is in need of money."

It was my turn to shake my head and smile. I opened my menu and skimmed the entrees. What in the world was seitan or tempeh? "What are you going to get?"

"I might try the truffled mushrooms and coconut bacon with the house flat bread."

Mushrooms weren't my favorite, so I couldn't play it safe and copy her order.

Our server approached with a smile and set down water with beaded condensation gripping the sides of the glasses. "Do you folks need a few more minutes, or are you ready to order?"

Nicole raised her brows in my direction.

"You go ahead."

As she told the server her choice, I scrambled to find a dish with ingredients I'd heard of before. I ate healthily, lots of fruits and vegetables, but I could safely say fermented bean curd had never touched my plate.

"And for you, sir?"

"Umm...I think I'll have the barbeque pulled jack-fruit tacos."

"I'll put this right in for you guys." She slipped her pen and pad of paper into her apron and walked over to a computer by the entrance of the kitchen.

Nicole's eyes seemed to laugh at me. "Big jackfruit fan, are you?"

"Sure. I eat it all the time." Never had it in my life.

"Uh huh. So, tell me. What exactly is a jackfruit, and what does it look like?"

I crossed my arms on the table and leaned forward. "Well, I don't know what the media has told you, but don't believe it. They have a political agenda."

"On jackfruit." She pushed her lips down when they obviously wanted to turn up.

I kept my face as serious as if I were delivering bad news to a patient. "Oh, yes. It's all a huge cover up."

"And what exactly are they trying to cover up?"

"How the fruit got its name, naturally."

She nodded along. "Naturally."

Getting her to play along with me was even more fun than pushing her buttons and getting a rise out of her. "See, Jackfruit got its name from the magic beans Jack planted. That beanstalk that grew to the giant in the clouds actually grew magic fruit. Jackfruit."

"Magic, huh?"

I nodded sagely. "After I eat the tacos, I'll be even more awesome than I already am."

Laughter bubbled from her mouth. An addictive

NICOLE   171

sound. Even if I lived a hundred more years, I wouldn't get tired of it or stop trying to hear her perfect pitch of amusement again.

"If that's your expectation from these tacos, you're going to be severely disappointed."

"Since when do tacos disappoint?"

She inclined her head to concede to my point.

"But even if they end up poisoning me," I spoke again, "it would be worth it to spend this evening with you."

She blushed and looked away. "I was right to warn Sierra about smooth-talking men."

My spine hit the seat back. "I'm not a smooth talker; I'm just not afraid to say what I really think."

Her face flushed deeper.

"I have to say, that shade of pink is very becoming on you."

She looked down at her dress—white with little blue flowers. "I'm not wearing pink."

I lifted a brow to my hairline, giving her a direct look. "Aren't you?"

She put her hands to her undoubtedly warm cheeks. "You should stop."

"Why?"

Her hands dropped to her lap. "Because I don't know when you're being serious or not."

I moved my foot until I found hers under the table, bumping her ankle so she'd look up at me. Her blue eyes held uncertainty. She may be sure about ways to make the world a better place, but I hadn't proved myself to her yet. I'd just have to work to put enough data in the pro column that she couldn't ignore the fact that we were good for each other.

"I've always been serious about you, Nicole. I just didn't always know it."

"Here we are." Our server approached with a tray laden with two hot plates. She placed our meals in front of us.

I let the heat of my gaze travel across the table. Some would probably think I wasn't playing it cool enough. That the things I'd said were too heavy and serious for a first date. And maybe they'd be right, but I didn't want Nicole to think I was only playing around. Not when I'd never been so earnest about something, or someone, in my life.

17

NICOLE

*T*he last time I'd been out on a date that I hadn't been bribed into going on, I'd still been married to Greg. His company always threw a swanky Christmas party, so we'd hired a babysitter to watch Sierra. Greg and I had been having problems, but he wanted to keep up pretenses. He said his coworkers didn't need to know about our private affairs. I agreed, so I purchased a red sheath dress with side ruching to try and slim my *problem areas.* Camille from the salon give me a sophisticated updo. Almost as soon as we entered the banquet hall, however, Greg excused himself. I was left standing with a flute of champagne I'd never drink in my hand. When Greg didn't come back, I went searching for him…and found him playing tonsil hockey in the coat closet with Chelsea from human resources.

"Something wrong?" Drew set down his fork and gave me his full attention.

Did he know how heady that was? To have someone so completely focused on me? I honestly didn't know what to do with the amount of attention he gave me. I'd try to divert his concentration, but an instinctual part of me knew my efforts would be futile.

Why me? Drew was successful, smart, funny, and extremely good looking, whereas I was overweight, divorced with a daughter, too opinionated, and somewhat abrasive. He could have any woman he wanted. Why had he chosen me?

"Nicole?" Concern entered his voice.

I blinked out of my self-deprecating thoughts and smiled at him. "Yes. Sorry. I'm fine." To prove it, I picked up my fork and took a bite. This restaurant really had earned all its positive Yelp reviews. Cashew cream garlic sauce swam with flavor, the fried sage adding a perfect note.

"How's the coconut bacon?" Drew's lips gave a wry twist. "I have to admire the ingenuity of vegans to use food in new ways."

I stabbed a piece with my fork. "It's really good. Do you want to try a bite?" I held the fork out between us.

Instead of taking the utensil from my hand, he half stood and leaned over the table, his fingers encasing my wrist to bring the fork to his mouth.

My gaze became captured by the movement, following the path until the bite disappeared past his teeth. I swallowed and worked my tongue over my lips, forcing out a, "Well?"

He chewed, considering. "It's salty, sweet, and crisp. I'm really surprised by how much it tastes like the real thing."

When he released my wrist, I could breathe again. "And how's your magic fruit?"

"The magic is how a fruit can have the same texture as pulled pork. It's some kind of voodoo." He wiped his mouth with his napkin. "I've been meaning to say how much I like your dress. Is that something you made yourself with the girls?"

I touched the halter straps at my collarbone. "You're looking at the reincarnation of a vintage bedsheet."

Ginger in food spiced things up. Eyes the same color trained on a person packed a punch as well. I felt the heat of his gaze all the way to my toes.

"You're incredible, you know that?"

I studied my now near-empty plate, out of my element. I'd never had the problem of not knowing what to say. No, my difficulty had always been in holding my tongue when others ran theirs. But this had to have been at least the fourth instance over the course of our dinner that I'd blushed—Me! Blushed!—and come up blank instead of having a witty retort.

I didn't know what to do with his undivided attention or with his compliments. I almost wished he'd say something stupid, like the dangers of oil pipelines were a hoax, so I could rant and dig into him about something I knew about. Something that didn't leave me feeling quite so shaken.

Our server placed a black check holder on our table. Drew pulled out his wallet and slipped a credit card in the little plastic flap at the top.

"Does Sierra have you on a strict curfew, or can I steal you away for a little while longer?"

I glanced at my watch. Dinner had taken less than an hour. While I didn't know exactly what to do with myself when Drew gave me his singular regard, I also didn't want to cut the night short. "I think she'd allow me a bit more time out."

"Good." He chuckled and replaced his credit card when the server returned it then stood.

"Where are we going?" I gathered my purse.

"If I told you that, I'd ruin the surprise."

"I'm not sure how many surprises I can take in one night."

He peered at me out of the corner of his eye as he held open the door for me to walk through. "Good thing I know mouth-to-mouth resuscitation then."

A mental picture of his mouth on mine, lips soft but firm, came into 3D focus. My chest tightened, imagining Drew's kiss. He seemed to do everything with deft precision. No reason to believe kissing would be any different. Would he touch my face? Cradle my cheek? Would the brush of his lips leave me wanting more or satisfy my every longing?

I snuck a glance at Drew. He smirked at me as if he

knew what his words had conjured up in my mind. The cad! This time I refused to look away. By sheer will I pushed down the rising heat climbing my neck and met his gaze head on.

Drew laughed and placed a hand on my lower back. "Come on." He led me back to his monstrosity of a gas guzzler and opened the door for me.

As he maneuvered along the roads, I looked out the passenger window. How had I found myself here? With Drew, no less. But maybe that was the wrong question to ask. Maybe the better question was, where did I see this thing going?

I had to be careful. Sierra had already grown attached to Drew, and if things didn't work out, her heart could be broken. We also shared friends. A break up could divide our little group. Look how things had turned out for Ross and Rachel. I didn't want to be the cause of conflict between Ben and Molly when they were so close to newly-wed bliss.

My palm tingled as fingers slipped across my skin and intertwined with my own. Drew's thumb caressed the back of my hand. "I'm not going to tell you to stop worrying, but do you want to share what's made you go quiet all of a sudden?"

I should've pulled my hand from his. Kept some sort of space between us while I still had a clear enough mind to do so. But instead I held on. If even for just this moment, I'd stop pretending I was stronger than I actually was. "I don't know if I can do this."

He waited a beat. "My driving isn't that bad. How hard can being a passenger be?"

His teasing loosened the band around my chest. "You know that's not what I meant."

He managed to turn the steering wheel without letting go of my hand. "What exactly are you worried about?"

A breath puffed out my cheeks. "Everything. We were oil and water before."

"Opposites attract all the time in nature," he reasoned calmly.

"And then there's the fact we share the same friends."

"Who are mature adults," he assured in his pacifying tone, understanding immediately my unspoken worry of an unfortunate outcome if we went past a first date and it didn't work out.

"But Sierra isn't." This sticking point. I had to make sure I made the right decision for both of us.

"No, she isn't," he agreed softly. Quiet overtook the inside of the Suburban.

That was it. The end before anything truly began. It was for the best.

If only the best didn't feel quite like the absolute worst.

Drew cleared his throat. "This probably isn't the best thing to say on a first date." His nervous chuckle vibrated with irony. "Running the risk of ruining everything, I'm just going to lay everything out on the table. No cards to my chest." He paused. "I like you, Nicole. I like you a lot."

A car passed us on the right. "You've made that pretty clear."

He squeezed my hand. "Good. But as much as I like you, I like Sierra even more."

Surprise unhinged my jaw.

"I'm kidding." He flashed me a wink before returning his attention to the road. "You know I can't have kids of my own, but if I could have a daughter, I'd want one like Sierra." His grip on my hand tightened. "This isn't coming out like I planned. I told you I wasn't a smooth talker."

My free hand covered his forearm. "What are you trying to say?"

He glanced at me, then flicked on his blinker light and pulled over on the side of the road, putting the vehicle in park. He turned his whole body toward me. "I know this is our first date, but I'm committed, Nicole. To both you and Sierra. This isn't a casual thing for me. I want a relationship with you that includes Sierra. A long-haul, our lives together, eventually a family type of relationship." His Adam's apple bobbed. "Is that okay or have I scared you off?"

I blinked at him, my mind a whirl of thoughts. "Yes."

He brushed my hair behind my shoulder, looking at me with a tenderness I'd never seen in someone's gaze. "Yes, it's okay, or yes, I scared you?"

My head tilted toward his hand. "Both."

His finger trailed my jaw. "I can live with that." He put the transmission into drive and merged back onto the road. When he pulled into a parking lot, I dropped my head to get a better view of the dark building with a domed roof.

"I think they're closed."

He killed the engine and pulled the keys out of the ignition. The door opened without him saying a word.

I exited the vehicle as well, but planted my feet. "I'm not prepared to add breaking and entering to my record."

The attractive tilt to his lips tugged me forward. "You have a record, do you?"

I shrugged. "I was in my early twenties and protesting against mining waste being dumped into the local waterways."

We approached a side door. Drew raised his hand and knocked. A minute later the door creaked open, revealing a woman in her mid-twenties with a badge on a lanyard around her neck.

"Hey, Veronica," Drew said.

"Good to see you, Drew." She opened the door wider so we could enter. "Everything is set up for you."

"Thanks." The door shut behind us.

Veronica turned in silhouette, and Drew stiffened slightly beside me before relaxing again. "I see congratulations are in order."

She placed a hand to her tiny baby bump, a glow in her cheeks. "Sixteen weeks."

Drew's hands dug into his pockets. "I'm happy for you."

Veronica dropped her chin. "Thank you."

My gaze bounced between them. Who was this woman to Drew?

She stopped in front of another door. "As I said, everything is set up. I'll leave you to it." With a small wave, she left.

I'd been so absorbed by their curious exchange, I hadn't even paid attention to where we were. Posters of constellations hung on the wall as well as a bust and plaque of Galileo.

"You brought me to the planetarium?"

He rocked back on his heels. "There's so much light pollution in the city, but I wanted to give you the stars."

I didn't even try to hold back my smile as I shook my head at him. "You and your lines."

He opened the door and escorted me in. A blanket and pillows had been set up on the floor near the middle of the circular room. We lowered ourselves to the blanket, and I ran my hand across the fleece, remembering the floor-is-lava incident. My life hadn't really been boring before Drew, but it had definitely become more fun and full of surprises since he'd entered the scene.

"You're probably curious about Veronica." His words pulled my head from the clouds—or the stars, rather, considering our location—and plunked me back in the present. Strange I could forget that little curiosity so quickly.

"She and I were engaged, once upon a time," he admitted.

Hold the phone. "She's the one who left you because you're infertile, and now she's pregnant!" My outraged voice echoed back to me.

Drew stretched his arms out to me, a big grin on his face. "Whoa. It's okay."

My nostrils flared. Now that I knew who Veronica was, I wanted to have a few words with her.

"Really, Nicole. It's okay. I couldn't give her everything she needed. She was right to end things when she did." He scooted toward me. "If she hadn't, I wouldn't be here with you now, and there's no place I'd rather be."

My spine melted. "Fine. I'll stow away my righteous indignation on your behalf."

He leaned forward, and I thought he might kiss me, but instead he ran the side of his finger down the slope of my nose. "Thank you." Standing, he walked to a console and pushed a few buttons. "Let's get this show started." The room plunged into darkness, then stars began to appear overhead.

The back of my eyes burned. No one had ever done anything so sweet or thoughtful before. Drew had not only set this whole thing up; he'd had to call the woman who'd broken his heart to do it. How could I doubt the validity of his earlier declaration when he'd gone to such lengths to make this night so memorable for me?

Drew sat beside me and arranged the pillows behind us. Once they'd been sufficiently fluffed, he lay down, and I followed his example.

The Milky Way burst in light and color against the black expanse. Purples and blues and whites. It was breathtaking, the beauty of creation. The largeness of the universe never ceased to make me more aware of how small I actually was, but also that my miniscule-ness didn't distract from my importance to the One who gave me life. That even set amongst the vastness of His creation, He cared enough to direct my steps.

A crick formed in my neck, so I wiggled, trying to get more comfortable without disturbing Drew.

His face turned toward me. "Something wrong?"

I stilled, my neck at an odd angle. He must have noticed because he lifted his arm closest to me and patted his chest in invitation with his other hand.

Dare I?

"I promise I won't bite."

It had been a long time since I'd been held. Greg had never been a cuddler, and I hadn't particularly wanted to snuggle up to him anyway. But Drew's shoulder looked so inviting. So did the soft look in his eyes.

I may regret this later. But that was future me's prob-lem. Present me scooted down and over and laid her cheek in the comfortable crook created by Drew's chest and shoulder. His heart beat a steady rhythm under my ear, and his shirt smelled earthy. Like sandalwood and the salt spray coming off the Pacific.

A contented sigh passed my lips, and I looked back up to stare at our galaxy.

Drew's finger glided up and down over the backside of my arm, causing gooseflesh to rise.

"I could get used to this," he murmured into my hairline.

Me too. "Have you ever seen stars this bright?" I asked, needing a distraction from the reaction my body had to him.

He nodded, and I felt the stubble on his jaw against my crown. "Up in Joshua Tree."

"I've heard they have good rock climbing."

His chest rumbled. No doubt his memory had brought up the same day mine had—the awful blind date with what's-his-name when the guy implied a harness wouldn't be able to fit around my hips and thighs. Who would have thought Drew and I would go from the heated words of that night to this?

"I was actually there for another reason."

"Hiking?"

"Not quite."

I leaned on my elbow to prop myself up so I could look at him. Our faces were inches apart, me hovering above him. My gaze fell to his lips. I watched, mesmerized as they parted then slowly arched upward.

He pushed himself up on his own elbow and faced

me. His smile fell in slow motion, the air between us fairly vibrating.

"Nicole." His voice held a deep, husky quality. "I'd really like to kiss you right now. May I?"

Whoever said asking for consent before a kiss wasn't romantic had never been asked by Drew Bauer.

Unable to form words, I simply nodded.

His eyes flashed, then darkened. His hand came up to rest against the side of my neck, his thumb at my jaw. He stroked my earlobe, sending tingles down my arm. "You're so beautiful," he whispered.

I licked my lips, my breath caught in my chest. When he angled my head for a better position, I didn't resist. I was putty in his hands. His face moved toward me, and my eyes slid shut.

His kiss was like nothing yet everything I'd imagined. Soft yet firm. Sweet yet heated. Leaving me craving more yet strangely satisfied. Stars may have been projected above us, but they flashed behind my eyes, shot through my body, and orbited around my heart.

It seemed to take all his strength to pull away, his breathing ragged. "Sorry, you were asking me why I was at Joshua Tree when I got distracted."

It took me a second to gather my composure. "I wasn't complaining."

He flashed me a devilish grin that made my stomach twist. "I'd gone during the government shutdown when they had to close the national park. Some idiots with chainsaws thought it would be funny to chop down the multiple-centuries-old trees, so I camped out for a few days."

"You were there to save the trees?"

He shrugged. "Technically they're not trees. They're—"

But I'd ceased listening and had lost the ounce of self-control I'd been clinging to. With a growl I didn't know I was capable of, I closed the distance between us, barely registering Drew's laugh as I claimed his lips with all the passion he'd asserted I possessed.

18

DREW

*G*inny opened the front door before I'd even had the chance to ring the doorbell. Her eyes were wide and slightly crazed as she reached forward and grabbed my arm, hauling me across the threshold and into her house.

"Whoa." I rubbed the back of my arm, even though it didn't really hurt. "Is everything all right?"

My sister threw her hands up in the air. "No, everything is *not* all right."

Brother and doctor instincts kicked into high gear. "Okay, calm down and tell me what's wrong."

Instead of following my advice by sitting in one of the comfortable spots in the living room, she began to pace.

"'Calm down,' he says." Her laugh held no humor. "So typical of a man. I'll forgive you, Drew, but only because I need you to do something for me."

She focused her gaze on me, a deranged glint in her eye, and I took a step back. I hadn't seen that look since we were children. After watching the winter Olympics, she'd convinced me to play bobsled. Our gold medal was a trip to the emergency room after our sled over-turned on the steep stairs and I rolled down head over heels, breaking my ulna.

"I need you to get it out, Drew." Her voice had gone calm, which should've made me feel better but only scared me more.

"Get what out?" I asked as if I were talking a jumper off the ledge.

She made a karate chop motion to the side of her rounded belly. "The baby. Get. It. Out."

I must have shrunk an inch as my body sagged. A relieved chuckle escaped my mouth.

Ginny's eyes flashed.

Right. No humor past the due date. "Ginny, you just made such a comfortable home in there that the little dude wants to stay a bit longer."

She huffed. "I don't care. Serve him his eviction notice."

"Have you tried everything your doctor suggested?"

"My feet hurt I've walked so much. I can't drink another cup of red raspberry leaf tea, and my stomach will revolt if I try to force more castor oil down. Plus, Eric's helped with all the recommendations on his end."

I held up a hand. "I don't need to hear about that."

"But the baby still hasn't come."

I wrapped my arm around her shoulders. "Trust your body. It's doing exactly what it's supposed to."

She pushed against my ribs and glared at me. "You're no help."

Eric came down the stairs. "Did she convince you to use the dining table as an OR to perform a C-section yet?" He grinned at Ginny.

"You're never touching me again," she said past gritted teeth.

"Food is ready," a third voice called from the back of the house where the kitchen was located.

"Mom's here?" I asked

"She made a tried and true labor-inducing eggplant parmesan. At least someone in my family is willing to help me." Her pointed look threw daggers at Eric and me.

"I hate to burst your bubble, sis, but Italian food doesn't induce labor."

Eric groaned. "Couldn't you have let her have this?"

She turned and planted a hand on her hip. "I'll have you know this is a famous recipe. The restaurant in Georgia that created the dish swears by its effectiveness. Over three hundred women have gone into labor within forty-eight hours after eating it, and I intend to be among their ranks."

Owen tried to barrel past on his way to the food, but Ginny's hand darted out and stopped him. "Wash up first."

He rolled his eyes, but trudged to the half bath off the hall.

The smell of fried food caused my stomach to growl. Leaving Ginny and Owen, I walked to the kitchen. Mom had on a ruffled apron over her Scooby-Doo scrubs. She must have come straight from the pediatric dentistry office. She turned, a bowl of spaghetti in her hands.

"Here, let me take that." I relieved her of the pasta, dropping a kiss on her cheek.

"So, I do have a second child. I was beginning to wonder if my memory was playing tricks on me and I'd been breaking and entering into a stranger's house to drop off meals."

I cringed and set the bowl on the table. "Sorry. I've been really busy lately."

The scolding expression she'd adopted for show vanished. Her mouth bowed, and her eyes brightened. "So I've heard."

Didn't need to call 811 before digging here. I could feel the underground current pulsing. "What does that mean?"

She transferred a green salad to the table. "Just that the hospital isn't the only place you've been seen at night, and patients aren't the only people you've been spending time with."

Veronica. I'd loved how close she'd become with my mom when we were together. Maybe not so much now. Parents should break up with exes the same time their children did.

"Drew went on a date?" Ginny interrupted. "An I'm-just-passing-the-time date or an actual, real, grown-up type of thing?"

"He called in a favor and got after-hours access to the planetarium." Mom beamed.

Ginny turned to me. "Who is she and why haven't we met her yet?"

Owen pulled out a chair, the feet scratching loudly against the floor.

"If we don't eat, I'm not sure your son will save any food for you, and then you may be pregnant forever without your magic eggplant parm."

An internal struggle took place behind Ginny's eyes. She clearly wanted to be nosey about my personal life, but she also desperately wanted to meet her new baby and not be pregnant anymore.

"Fine," she conceded on a burst of wind. "But don't think you're off the hook."

Eric said grace at the head of the table, then we began passing plates around. Conversation turned to Eric's job, and I was more than content to hand over the spotlight to him. With less people grilling me about Nicole, I could eat in peace. I didn't know about the validity of the breaded and fried vegetable topped with tomato sauce to induce labor, but it sure tasted good.

Owen tilted to the side, the sound of flatulence cutting into the conversation around the table.

"Owen!" Ginny reprimanded.

The boy grinned but said, "Excuse me."

I reached over to him under the table and tapped knuckles with him with a wink.

"Does anyone need a refill?" Ginny asked as she pushed away from the table.

"I'll get it, sweetheart." Eric moved to stand, but Ginny waved him off.

"I need to stretch anyway." She picked up her glass and waddled into the kitchen.

Crash!

Shattered glass mixed with a startled cry.

"Ginny." Eric knocked over his chair in his haste to rush to his wife's side.

She stood still, breathing hard. "My water broke."

"It's time?"

Their gazes locked. "It's time."

As if a starting gun at a race had been shot, Eric took off. He rounded the corner and jogged up the stairs two at a time. Mom and I picked our way into the kitchen. I collected large chunks of broken glass while Mom retrieved the broom from the closet.

The ceiling reverberated under Eric's stomping around. He came down the stairs holding a small suitcase. "Why are you still standing there?" he panted to Ginny.

Ginny looked down at herself. "I'm not going like this."

"What are you talking about, woman?" Now Eric appeared the crazed one.

Ginny used the countertop to support her weight. "Don't 'woman' me. And I mean I'm not walking out in public looking like I wet myself."

"But...but...it's time," Eric stuttered.

"Owen took fourteen hours to make his appearance. I think I can take a couple of minutes to put on clean clothes and maybe a maxi pad so I don't keep leaking on myself."

Mom set the broom aside. "Eric, help your wife up the stairs and into something more comfortable. We'll get the car ready for you."

Her no-nonsense mother tone snapped something in my brother-in-law. He wrapped his arm around Ginny's back and supported her on the slow trek up the stairs.

I tossed the contents of the dust pan in the trash and turned to find Owen munching on a piece of garlic bread.

"Glad to see your appetite hasn't been affected."

He shrugged and took another bite.

By the time I'd finished mopping up the floor, Ginny and Eric stood at the base of the stairs.

"Drew?" Ginny's gaze held a question.

I gave her a gentle hug. "Go. I'll hold down the fort. I know you'd rather have Mom there than your brother, even if I *am* a doctor."

Her body stiffened, and she sucked in a breath. She waited until the contraction passed. "Thank you."

I gave her a miniscule shove. "Go bring another terrific nephew into the world for me."

Once they'd gone, I turned to Owen. "Want to play Xbox?"

"Will you play Minecraft with me?"

"Sure."

He set the game up and handed me a controller. "Survival or creative?"

"Let's start in creative. We can mine and build everything we need before switching to survival."

The world generated, then Owen teleported my boxy character Steve to his character's location. Owen built a crafting table and started moving ingredients to basic recipes to create building material. I clicked on dirt and started placing blocks in a row.

"Only newbs build with dirt, Uncle Drew."

"My bad." I clicked into my inventory.

"You're dating Sierra's mom, aren't you?"

My thumb hit the B button too hard. "Why do you think that?"

He focused on the game. "I'm nine, not blind."

Well, all right then.

"She's cool."

My neck craned in his direction. "Nicole?"

"Sierra." He didn't bother looking over at me. "I'm just saying, if I'm getting a cousin that's not a boy, I like Sierra well enough. At least she can play football."

I laughed under my breath then reached over and tousled his hair.

What would Nicole think of meeting my family? She hadn't freaked out when I told her I was all in. Opposite actually, as we'd shared so much of ourselves —including kisses—beneath the projected stars. I wanted to move forward, but I didn't want to scare her in the process.

19

NICOLE

*K*aty Perry's "Roar" filtered through the salon's speakers. Camille swayed to the beat at the front, straightening the product display as she lip-synced to the lyrics.

"Belt it out, girl," I told her. "There's no one here but us." A lull in walk-ins and no reservations gave us both a nice break.

Amanda, sitting in my salon chair, looked up from her phone. "Hey," she protested my use of the words *no one.*

Camille curled her fingers like claws and roared as if she were a wild cat.

I spun Amanda in the chair. "I included you in the *us,* silly."

She focused her gaze on me as her body rotated in a tight circle, whipping her head around to refocus like a ballerina would to not get dizzy. Once the chair slowed, she returned to tapping on her screen. "Thank you."

I sighed. With the amount of time Amanda sat in front of screen, she'd be blind by forty. I rummaged through my purse and pulled out an eye-glass case. Popping it open, I unfolded a pair of bright yellow blue-light-blocking frames and handed them to Amanda. "Use these. I can't let you damage your retinas."

She accepted my glasses and slid them to perch on her nose. "Nicole the Protector to the rescue."

"I'm not exactly a superhero like Diana Prince."

"Sure you are."

"How, do you think?"

"She's from the Amazon." Amanda shrugged. "You want to save the Amazon."

I rested my hip on the half counter holding my hair dryer, clippers, and other tools of my trade. "One is a mythical island and the other is a rainforest responsible for producing six percent of the world's oxygen as well as absorbing large quantities of carbon dioxide from the atmosphere."

"See? Totally the same thing." She grinned.

I shook my head at her.

She pocketed her phone, winced, and touch her temple.

"Headache?"

Her blue eyes blinked then cleared. "It's nothing."

I grabbed a brush from a drawer and moved to stand behind her.

"What are you doing?"

"Stop being so suspicious and relax." I released the hair tie holding her ponytail in place and let her long brown locks flow over the back of the chair. Starting at the bottom in case there were any snags, I ran the brush through her hair. After a few minutes, when the bristles ran over her scalp, Amanda sighed.

"That feels good, thank you."

"You're welcome." Long, even strokes from the crown to the tip drained stress from her muscles. "Straight talk?"

She peeked at me out of one eye.

"Where were you the other day? Not that I expect you at Sierra's games or anything, but you'd said you'd be there, then you weren't." My hand stilled. "I just want to make sure that you're okay."

If I hadn't been looking, I'd have missed the flinching of her fingers on the armrest along with the slight downturn of her mouth.

Was something going on in Amanda's life that she hadn't shared with me or any of the other girls? Why would she feel the need to keep secrets from us?

The front door opened, the outside breeze catching and blowing in a familiar scent. One of clean soap and freshly mowed lawns. Of Friday night lights and lazy weekend mornings. Of warm hugs and scintillating kisses.

Our gazes collided in the mirror. My lips tingled, remembering the last time Drew and I had spent time together. Heat infused my cheeks...then spread south-ward throughout the rest of my body.

"Interesting," Amanda drawled, widening my frame of mind to more than one point. One man.

I glanced at Amanda, but what could I say? Not that long ago I'd never have thought in a million years that there'd be anything between Drew and me but animosity.

I hadn't judged the book by its cover—there wasn't a thing wrong with Drew's cover, if you know what I mean—but the pages he showed the world weren't the complete story. There was so much more to him than he let most people see. Yes, he liked to play games, but I trusted him not to play games with my heart.

"Welcome back." Camille walked to the front counter. "Are you in need of another cut?"

"Umm..." Drew looked past Camille to me, his brows rising in silent supplication.

"This conversation isn't over," I whispered to Amanda out of the side of my mouth.

She laughed and set my glasses on the half counter-top. "Doesn't look like I'm the one needing to spill. Better get your story in order in the next couple of hours, because the spotlight will be on you tonight, Wonder Woman." She sauntered toward the front of the salon. "Hey, Drew."

He dipped his chin. "Amanda."

Her gaze roamed over his hair, her knowing grin widening before she walked out of the salon.

He touched his temple, looking at me for help again.

"I'll take him, Camille."

My coworker's hand paused over the POS monitor. "You sure?"

Pins and needles pricked the tips of my fingers. I curled them into my palms. My fingers threaded through people's hair every day. There had never been anything sensual about the act. Long, short, coarse, fine, curly, or straight. It was just a job. Or it had been. Nothing after Drew took my seat would be professional. It couldn't be after the other night.

My breath caught as he walked toward me. Silly, really. We'd already kissed. All the build-up and anticipation should have passed. The wonder and expectancy. But if anything, all those pre-kiss marvels only intensified. Because now I knew. I knew what his lips softly pressed against mine felt like. What they ignited deep in my core. And now that I'd had a taste, I wanted more. Feared that perhaps I could never have enough.

His eyes slipped down to my mouth, and I felt the weight of his regard on my lips. His gaze felt like a caress even when he didn't touch me.

He stopped, the chair between us, and his eyes rose to mine. How had I ever thought this man shallow? A person could drown in his depths.

"I missed you." His voice sounded deeper.

Missed me when we'd seen each other only two days before. Committed to me when we'd only gone out the one time. His words worked like salve over wounds I hadn't known still festered. I'd thought I'd healed after Greg's betrayal and abandonment, but my soul soaked up Drew's declarations like the cracked ground of a desert soaks up the oft-prayed-for rain.

Though relationships were scary, even more so after the hurt of a failed one, I'd never been a person to shy from the hard things in life. And so I voiced the honesty of my heart, the knowledge of which transferred the same amount of power and vulnerability his admission had handed me. "I missed you, too."

He smiled. Not his cocky grin. Not his I'm-messing-with-you smirk. Not his boyish tilt of the lips. No. This smile was different than he'd flashed me before. Deeper. Brighter. Fuller. As if he were smiling with his whole heart.

I gripped the back of the salon chair for stability.

"I'm sorry I didn't call last night."

Ha. Maybe I should apologize for not waiting by the phone. It had been so long since I'd really dated that I'd forgotten the protocols.

"My sister went into labor, so I was on uncle duty."

"How is she doing?"

His smile morphed into the mushy expression one can only get when thinking of babies. "Mom and baby are both doing well."

"Another nephew, or niece this time?"

"A boy. Isaac. They stuck with the vowel theme."

I remembered the mention of his nephew, Owen, but hadn't known there was a whole theme. "Oh?"

"My brother-in-law is named Eric, then my nephew Owen, and now Isaac."

"Can I see a picture?"

He pulled out his phone faster than a wrangler at a draw at high noon on the O.K. Corral. He tapped on the screen a few times, then handed me the device. A ruddy baby with a smooshy face, all swaddled and wearing a soft knit hat filled the screen. I looked up at Drew then back at the picture. "He has your chin."

Drew brightened even more. "You think?"

I handed his phone back. "Definitely."

"I was on my way there now to see them but wanted to stop by here first. I missed you."

I didn't think I'd ever smiled as much as I did when I was with Drew. "You said that already."

He didn't appear sheepish or embarrassed. Just gazed at me in that tender way of his. "It needed to be repeated."

My chest swelled, and I bit down on the inside of my bottom lip. Drew put me out of sorts. I worked on facts and battle plans. I didn't know what to do with the flood of feelings his words and attention rained down upon me.

I dropped my gaze to the chair to regain my equi-

librium. "Guess you don't need a haircut after all then."
I peeked back up at him.

His flirtatious smile was back in full force. "As
much as I want your hands on me, I'll have to take a
raincheck."

His insinuation shot flames up my neck and sent an
ache to my belly. I was a mother, not some naive,
untried, green miss—or however someone in Jane
Austen's day would describe a virgin. Drew's words
may have been innocent and teasing, but it had been a
long time since anyone wanted to touch me in a physically intimate way.

The echo of the Shulamite's advice to the daughters
of Jerusalem rang in my head. *I adjure you, O daughters
of Jerusalem, do not stir up or awaken love until it is ready!*
Whether she meant emotionally, physically, or both, I
didn't know, but I tucked the warning into the corner
of my heart.

"I'll see you at the game tomorrow night." Drew
stepped forward and pressed his lips to my cheek.
"Bye."

My hand rose to my waist, and I gave him a
small wave as he exited the salon. I rotated my
chair to face me and sank into the seat. I'd always
known Drew was trouble. I just hadn't realized the
trouble would be to my heart. But there was no way
around the situation. Someone had found a remote
control to our relationship and pushed the fast
forward button. What other explanation could there

be when I found myself already half in love with the man?

I went through the motions of the rest of the work day, giving a sailor a high and tight and working through my afternoon balayage appointment. "I'll see you tomorrow," I called to Camille as I clocked out.

Sierra had asked if she could spend the night at a friend's house, and since they didn't have school in the morning, because it was a teacher in-service day, I'd given her permission.

After driving through some traffic, I pulled off to the side of the street in front of Jocelyn and Molly's house. The duo had been hosting our sewing circle since the beginning, and their house was a sort of oasis for me. A safe place outside the craziness of the real world. Although, remembering Amanda's warning from earlier, I wasn't sure how safe it would be tonight.

I turned off the engine and made a grab toward the bag of sewing supplies I kept in the passenger seat. Only they weren't there. Right. Because we had the dresses for the wedding to finish. Instead, I slung my purse over my shoulder and stepped out of the car. The front door of the house opened, and Amanda spilled out. I braced, knowing my best friends were going to reenact the Spanish Inquisition on me.

Amanda laid ahold of my wrist when I neared and pulled me into the house. "We've been waiting for you."

"So I see," I said dryly.

She dragged me into the living room, where I

expected a darkened room with a spotlight and maybe some swirling cigarette smoke like in a noir film but instead found my friends swathed in Molly's wedding colors of soft yellow and white.

Molly stood in the center in her gorgeous hand-made creation, looking like the cover of a bridal magazine. Jocelyn had on her bridesmaid gown, an off-the-shoulder flowing number with a chiffon overlay. Betsy's arms were crossed over a sweetheart neckline, the lines of her gown hugging her curves in a mermaid silhouette with a slit up to her knee. She looked equal parts rock-and-roll and girl-next-door.

Jocelyn held a tea-length dress up to me in one hand. "Go try this on." She pushed my shoulders, directing me to the bathroom.

Amanda picked up her own dress from the back of the couch and headed down the hall to change in one of the bedrooms.

I shimmied out of my jeans and blouse, then slipped the dress over my head. The illusion neckline covered my chest in a see-through frothy material. The skirt of the dress belled out in thick layers of tulle. I couldn't believe the reflection looking back at me in the mirror. Jocelyn had somehow managed to get each of our personalities in her designs.

I stepped out of the bathroom, colliding with Amanda in the hall. Her dress was a simple sleeveless A-line, fully ruched bodice with a charmeuse band flowing into a tea-length hemline.

We stood in a sorry excuse for a circle, staring at each other.

"I'm getting married," Molly breathed.

"I'm moving," Jocelyn announced without preamble.

"Nicole's dating Drew," Amanda nearly shouted.

We blinked at each other, absorbing the trio of declarations. Of course, I'd been aware of two out of the three, but Jocelyn's news made my head spin.

"You're moving?" I said at the same time as Jocelyn squawked, "You're dating Drew?"

Molly clapped her hands. "Who cares if I'm getting married? I'm so excited for you guys!"

Betsy harrumphed. "I feel like squealing may ensue, so I'm going to exit stage left now." She started unzipping her dress as she walked toward the hall.

Molly turned to Jocelyn. "I'm guessing you're moving to be closer to Malachi?"

Jocelyn nodded, her complexion fairly glowing with contentment. "The long-distance thing isn't working anymore. I want to be with him all the time, not just a few days a month."

Amanda clasped her fingers together in front of her. "I can't believe you're leaving. What about us? We'll never see you again."

I frowned at Amanda. "She's moving a few hours away, not dying. Of course we'll see her again."

Jocelyn's smile held a hint of sadness. "You can't get rid of me that easily. I plan on driving down at least once a month, and you all can come up to see me too."

"But things will be different. Our group won't be the same." Amanda picked at her dress, not meeting anyone's gaze.

"There are such things as Facetime, Skype, and Zoom," Molly soothed. "We'll set up a computer during our sewing sessions so Jocelyn can still be with us."

Betsy returned wearing a tee that said *Please don't interrupt me while I'm ignoring you.* "Have we passed the 90210-drama phase, or do I need to give you guys five more minutes?"

Jocelyn stood at Betsy's side and wrapped her arms around the snarky Argentinian. "I'm going to miss you, too."

Betsy patted Jocelyn's arm in a *there, there* gesture.

Jocelyn let her go and turned to me. "Now, what's this about Drew? You guys finally stopped dancing *around* each other and started dancing *with* each other?"

"You should have seen the looks that passed between them earlier." Amanda cackled. "I thought I would need to call the fire department to put out the heat of their gazes."

Betsy fell onto the sofa. "I'm not sure why the three of you are making such a big deal about them. We all knew they'd get together months ago."

"And I'm not sure if I should thank you or be offended," I said dourly.

Betsy shrugged like she couldn't care either way.

"I want to know when you finally saw what we all

did." Molly gingerly lowered herself onto the sofa, making sure not to crush her gown.

"There wasn't a single moment. Not like I'd been in a dark room and someone all of a sudden turned on a light. More like the gradual lightening of dawn, a little at a time, until I recognized what stood before me."

"A new day," Molly sighed.

Jocelyn squeezed my hand. "A new beginning."

"A brighter tomorrow," Amanda added.

Betsy crossed her arms. "Don't expect me to chorus in on this nauseating display. You guys can be sickeningly sweet on your own."

Amanda, Molly, Jocelyn, and I all looked at each other, our thoughts in harmony. As one, we converged on Betsy, smothering her in a group hug she groused about.

Some things did change. Like new relationships or new addresses, but other things would never change. Like us. We'd always stay the best of friends.

20

DREW

*T*he Earth's dome overhead darkened in shades of navy and grey, the high watt LED lights spilling their brilliance onto the football field. Only seconds left on the play clock, and the results of this last play would be the difference between the kids leaving the game with their spirits resembling the darkening sky or the bright lumens of the broad-beamed floodlights.

I'd called a time out, and the team huddled around me. If there'd been any sort of chill in the air, their breaths would've been seen in the circle. As it was, the panting from eleven kids filled the small space in front of our scrunched bodies.

Sierra wedged her hand above her face mask to wipe at the sweat beading on her forehead. Her flushed cheeks and obvious fatigue attested to the amount of game she'd played.

I glanced back at Tommy on the bench. His throw wasn't as accurate and he didn't have the power in his arm that Sierra did, but he was fresh. I could call a short pass or even a running play. Get our man out of bounds to stop the clock. Maybe we'd have a chance.

I looked back at Sierra, but she'd taken her focus off me. She stared over my shoulder, her eyes wide and her jaw unhinged. I turned slightly to follow her line of sight and saw a man walking down the small hill from the parking lot to the field. Who was the guy to get that sort of reaction from Sierra?

There was literally no time to contemplate the mystery man. The referees would blow the whistle signaling the end of our time out, and I needed to give the team a play to execute.

"Sierra."

At the sound of her name she dragged her eyes back to me. She must have seen an apology on my face. Anticipated my words.

"Don't take me out, Coach Drew. Please."

I reached out and laid my hand on her shoulder pad. "You've played an amazing game, but maybe we let Tommy have a turn."

A desperation filled her eyes, so much like her mother's in shape rather than color. "Please," she begged. "My dad just got here. He's never seen me play."

My gaze snapped back to the new arrival. He'd made it to the pack of parents camping out along the opposite sideline He wore a pair of khaki Dockers and a blue polo. Boat shoes with no socks. That was Sierra's dad, Nicole's ex?

An unfamiliar something coiled just below my ribs, snaking around my chest cavity and squeezing until I thought a bone would break. My feet urged me to move. To eat up the ground that separated us like a bulldozer flattens the dirt. My fingers curled in on themselves. An unsatisfied impulse to let this pent-up compression in my body out through my fists.

"Coach Drew." This time it was Sierra's sweet voice pulling me back to the huddle. Her eyes still held that sheen of desperation, but also a strength I'd recognized in her mother. Determination.

Part of me crumbled. No eight-year-old should have to fight to prove *anything* to one of their parents. Love should be unconditional. Stable. Reliable. But here a girl stood, exhausted but unwilling to rest because she thought she had to earn a place in her father's life and in his heart.

It was on my lips to say no. Greg didn't deserve this brilliant girl as a daughter, and she shouldn't have to perform to earn his attention. But I couldn't make my tongue form the words. I couldn't be the cause of her face falling or disappointment extinguishing the light in her eyes.

"Okay," I said, wanting nothing more than to crush her to my chest. Protect her the way her father should. I tore my gaze away, focusing on Maddox.

"Get open and run like the wind. I formation, out and up."

The whistle blew, and the offensive players ran back to the line of scrimmage, arranging themselves into I formation. Sierra called hike, and the center snapped the ball between his legs. She danced in the pocket, looking for an open player to pass the ball to. But all the receivers were blocked. A defensive lineman broke a tackle and charged. Sierra tucked the ball safely to her side and sprinted through an opening. Past the line of scrimmage, she had no choice but to run the ball.

My heart squeezed. I'd never asked Sierra to run the ball. Ever. In the pocket she could be sacked, true. But past offensive linemen, she had no protection. I wished I were standing beside Nicole. Holding her hand in support. She'd been nervous to let Sierra play in the first place. Watching her daughter run a gauntlet through players wanting nothing more than to stop her by physical force must be giving her a heart attack.

The safety on the other team ran a line straight toward Sierra, arms pumping and legs carrying him quickly over the field. A third player came out of my peripheral vision, clad in our red jersey. Number ten. Owen. Head down, he sprinted up the middle of the field. Would he intercept the other team's player to block him? Would the safety plow into Sierra before she reached the end zone? Would she be okay?

New rules and safety precautions arose every year

to keep players from injury, but football was still a contact sport. Sprains, broken bones, and even concussions happened every year.

If something happened to Sierra, I'd never forgive myself. Then again, Nicole would probably kill me anyway. Nothing less than I'd deserve.

Closer the three players came, a shrinking triangle. Then, *crash!* The unmistakable sound of colliding bodies. Sierra, Owen, and the safety all fell in a rolling heap. Two refs ran over. One raised his hands over his head in the touchdown signal and the other blew his whistle. Game over.

As the illuminated numbers on the scoreboard changed to show our win, I raced to the end zone. Owen and the other team's player rolled and slowly stood, but Sierra lay still.

Too still.

My heart dropped as my lungs forgot how to work. What other explanation could there be for my inability to draw breath?

I fell to my knees at Sierra's side. My fingers shook as I unclasped the chin strap and pulled her helmet off.

"Sierra." My voice echoed in my ears. "Sierra, sweetheart, can you hear me?"

Her face turned to me, a smile playing at the corners of her mouth. "Did my dad see me?"

Forget her deadbeat father! I pressed my lips together and looked over to the line of parents. Nicole ran toward us, but Greg had his phone pressed against his ear. Even when he was here, he wasn't present.

I forced the muscles in my face to relax before I looked back down at Sierra. "Of course he did. No one could have missed that play."

Her grin widened, but she still didn't make a move to stand.

"How are you? Anything hurting?"

She shook her head and finally sat up. "Just had the wind knocked out of me is all."

Nicole fell to her knees beside us and wrapped her arms around her daughter, pulling Sierra to her chest. She ran her hand down Sierra's sweaty hair and pressed a kiss to her temple. Cupping her face, she pushed Sierra slightly away and looked into her eyes. "Are you okay? What were you thinking? Goodness, Grandma might have been right, and we can't have that." Tears brimmed her bright blue eyes. "You were amazing, sweetie. Simply amazing."

"Thanks, Mom."

Nicole looked at me for the first time. "Now, check her to make sure she doesn't have a concussion," she demanded.

I'd already done a mental check. Sierra had looked up to me with a steady gaze, and the floodlights were behind me, so she wasn't sensitive to light. She'd risen on her own and had done so without any problems, so I didn't think she had any dizziness or balance issues. She didn't seem nauseous, dazed, or stunned.

"Nicole…" I started to reassure her.

She pinned me with a look as effective as a world wrestler pinning her opponent to the mat. "Check. Her."

Nicole's arms were full of Sierra. Since I couldn't reach out and touch her, I looked at her with a caress in my gaze. "Of course." Shifting my eyes downward, I focused on Sierra. "Any headache? Drowsiness? Does your brain feel foggy or do you feel unnaturally sleepy? Numbness or tingling anywhere?"

"No." Sierra shook her head. "I feel fine."

I met Nicole's eyes. Her mouth pinched, but she seemed satisfied. She got to her feet, and Sierra and I followed suit.

"Your dad is waiting to say hi." Nicole pointed to the sidelines. Sierra ran off. Yep, no balance issues whatsoever.

Surprise shocked me more than the contact to my upper arm. My hand went to cover the spot on reflex, though the small punch hadn't hurt, and I doubted it was meant to. I turned back to Nicole.

"What was that for?" Hopefully I'd kept enough of the chuckle out of my voice to not earn me a second punch. It had been a while since Nicole had looked at me with her blue eyes sparking like the hottest part of a fire. Reminded me why I'd loved to goad her in the first place.

Too bad we weren't somewhere more private…

"You put my baby in danger," she accused.

I ran my hand over the back of my neck. "She wasn't supposed to run the ball. She noticed her dad, and I think—"

Nicole cut me off with a raised hand. "I'm sure I can guess what she thought."

We both watched father and daughter at the edge of the field.

"So that's your ex." An inane statement if ever there was one.

She shoved her hands in her pockets. "Yep." Her dejected air did something to me. Sierra wasn't the only one I wanted to protect, though Nicole was more than capable.

I stepped a little closer, my chin inches from her ear. "His loss is my gain."

She smiled up at me, a little tremulous. "I should probably get over there."

I forced myself to take a step back. "I'll see you later."

"But not soon enough." She met my gaze for two beats before turning and walking back to Sierra and Greg. Two beats in which hope seeped past any doubts and uncertainties. I wasn't alone in my feelings. Wasn't moving faster, leaving her behind in the friend zone while I galloped to something more. We were running together, toward each other. Toward a lasting future.

Feeling light, I made my way back to the coach's sideline and began gathering up the cones and balls we'd used to warm up before the game. Everything in the mesh bag, I slung the supplies over my shoulder and headed to the parking lot. A lone figure where the parents congregated pulled my attention to the side.

I should leave him there. Pass by without saying anything. Why, then, did my feet take me in his direction?

Greg watched me approach, a pleasant expression on his face. Stranger meeting stranger. Except we weren't strangers. Not really. I knew him as the pain of Nicole's past. The baggage she carried around. I knew him as the shadow in Sierra's eyes. The one man she should always be able to count on but couldn't.

Those two ladies had come to mean more to me in a short amount of time than was probably logical. But the heart was not always logical, and that irrational organ propelled me toward the source of so much of my ladies' pain.

"Great game, Coach." Greg held out his hand to shake mine in congratulations.

I stared at his limb in disgust. "Did you even see more than ten seconds of it?"

His hand fell as his brows rose. "Excuse me?"

I adjusted my grip on the mesh bag. "You heard me. Did you see more than ten seconds of the game? Or the previous game? Or the one before that?"

"That's really none of your—"

"You have a wonderful daughter, if you don't know. Maybe you should try carving out some of your precious time to spend with her."

Red climbed Greg's neck. "Who are you to tell me anything about my daughter?"

My toes inched closer to his personal space. "Someone who's spent more time with her than her own father. Maybe even someone who cares about her more than you do."

His nostrils flared, and his gaze widened past me. "Tell Sierra I'll call her. I'm not going to stand here and take this from some volunteer county coach who doesn't have anything better to do than insert himself where he doesn't belong."

"Greg." Nicole rushed past me, a quiver in her voice I'd never heard before. "Wait. Sierra will be out in one second. Will you just wait?"

Greg didn't wait. He didn't even slow as he marched his way to his sports car and peeled out of the parking lot.

Nicole spun on her heel. Any defeat in her posture had been replaced with an iron rod. "You had no right." Her voice quaked with an entirely different emotion.

I held my hands out. "Nicole."

"No." She slashed at the air. "Do you have any idea how hard I worked just to get him here in the first place? He was going to take Sierra to get ice cream to celebrate her victory. How do you think that little girl is going to feel when she comes out here and sees her father gone? Again."

A boulder sank in my stomach. "We can take her for ice cream." It wasn't the same. I knew that. And nothing I did would reverse time and allow me to take back my words. I didn't regret saying them, and Greg needed to hear that and more, but the person to suffer for my lack of control would be Sierra, and I never wanted that.

Some of the vinegar evaporated from Nicole's expression. "Look, I know you meant well." She shook her head and looked to the side. "But it wasn't your place."

My wrist rotated to set the balls at my feet. "Where is my place, Nicole?"

She screwed her lips tight. Shook her head again.

I took a tentative step toward her. "I want my place to be with you and Sierra."

She looked at me then, eyes full of regret. "We don't always get what we want," she whispered, voice strangled.

I stilled. "What does that mean?"

Her shoulders rose and fell. Where was the woman with the fighting spirit? The one who tried to save an entire planet singlehandedly?

"I don't know." She sounded defeated. "What I do know is I need to call Greg and try to smooth this over. I need to check on Sierra and see if she's finished changing and break it to her gently that her dad bailed yet again. And I need to be there and help her through another disappointment."

She made to move past me, but I reached out and touched her arm. I wanted so desperately to help lift the weight off her shoulders, but she had to allow me close enough to do that. While I'd stated my desire to be by her and Sierra's sides, it felt as if she was pushing me away.

I let my hand slide to her fingers and squeezed. "I'm sorry, Nicole. If you need space, I'll respect that, but you aren't the only one who knows how to fight for something."

She didn't squeeze my hand back. "I'll call you later," she said.

Once more I was left watching her walk away from me.

NICOLE

"*Really*, Mom?" Sierra gave me an unamused expression, exasperation fairly dripping from her tilted head.

We'd entered some kind of Freaky Friday body switch scenario where she looked and sounded like the mother while I was the one standing as a child under her chastisement.

And I felt properly reproved. Not that I needed her to tell me the same things I'd been telling myself.

I'd acted too hastily. Spoken too harshly. Walked away too quickly.

"You need to apologize," she stated as a matter of fact.

I bit my lip.

Her eyes narrowed. "It's what you'd make me do." Some of her rigidness loosened. "Besides, Mr. Drew didn't say anything that wasn't true or that you didn't wish you could say. Dad really isn't winning any Father of the Year awards."

I pointed a silent reprimand her way.

"What? I'm not being disrespectful. Just stating things as they are."

"Toeing the line." Not that she was wrong or I hadn't thought the same, but I didn't want my sour thoughts about the man to bleed onto our daughter.

She rolled her eyes. "Fine. But you will apologize, won't you?"

I sighed. "Grownup things aren't always so simple."

"Or maybe grownups just like to make things more complicated," she muttered under her breath.

Again, not wrong.

But before I saw Drew again, I needed to figure out a few things. Not about him—he couldn't have been clearer on where he stood. Or where he'd like to stand, rather. By my side, committed to something lasting.

The problem was, it had been just Sierra and me together for so long. Could I make room for another person?

Haven't you already? The answer whispered like the faint scent of roses on a summer's breeze.

I'd never needed a knight to scale my walls, and Drew didn't really fit that heroic description. He was more a court jester, making me laugh when was too serious or had no reason for amusement.

Either way, he'd infiltrated my life…and my heart, if I were honest. Little by little until he'd expanded my borders to make room for himself. So the question wasn't whether there was space for Drew; the question was whether I wanted him to stay and allowed him into every corner of my life.

The yes reverberating around my skull had the volume of a megaphone behind it. A smile tickled my lips. I needed to find Drew and tell him his place was right by my side.

Sierra's arms were folded over her chest as she watched me.

Pretty sure I knew the answer to this, but... "What do you think of Mr. Drew having a, uh, not a permanent—not yet anyway—but, uh, a more fixed, yeah fixed, place in our lives?"

Sheesh. That could have gone more smoothly.

"Are you asking me how I feel about you two dating for real?" Her eyes said *duh*, but thankfully she didn't vocalize her thoughts on what she obviously perceived as an obtuse question on my part.

"Well, yeah."

"Mom." Her voice said it all. Slightly exasperated, as if she couldn't even believe I'd asked.

What had happened to my sweet eight-year-old, and how had this sassy-pants teenage wannabe take her place?

I pulled her into a hug. At this rate, I probably didn't have too many more years before she'd be too "cool" for such displays.

"So you're going to talk to him?" There was my little

girl, excitement shining from her eyes.

"Yes, I'm going to talk to him," I reassured her. My life wasn't the only one Drew had charmed his way into.

"Good." She picked up my car keys and handed them to me.

"Now?" I laughed as she physically pushed me to the door.

"You're always telling me not to put off to tomorrow what I can do today. Plus, Mrs. Crabtree from next door said she'd watch me."

I put my hand on the door jamb to stop Sierra from pushing me all the way out of doors. "When did she say that?"

A mischievous twist curled her mouth. Not unlike a certain someone else. "When I asked her twenty minutes ago."

I stepped off the porch. "Okay, but when I get back, we're going to have a talk about boundaries, young lady."

She grinned. "Sure, Mom."

"And lock the house before you head next door," I directed over my shoulder.

Sierra waved as I pulled out of the driveway. What did it mean that I knew where to find Drew? That his schedule had somehow been added to the many lists regulating my days?

If I hadn't already realized how far past the starting line we were in our relationship, this alone should've solidified the standing. Casual couples couldn't pinpoint the other on a Monday afternoon without a check in. Nor did they break traffic laws in their haste to see the other person.

In record time, I found myself pulling into a parking spot in the garage adjacent to Mercy Hospital. I wouldn't keep him away from his patients for long. Just a few minutes to tell him I didn't want anyone, especially my ex-husband, coming between us. If I could find a supply closet for a few stolen moments to punctuate my declaration, all the better.

I found a directory, then made my way to Drew's department and stopped at the front desk. "Is Dr. Bauer in? I don't have an appointment but wanted to speak with him for just a moment."

The receptionist eyes me warily. "I'm sorry, but I can't give out that kind of information."

"Oh." Bother. I pulled out my phone. "I don't want to get you into trouble or anything. Drew and I are friends you see." I rotated my phone to show her I had his name and number in my contact list. "I'd call, but I was kind of hoping to surprise him."

The woman looked like she'd worked a long day. She stared at my phone then peered back up into my face. Finally, she leaned back in her swivel chair. "Not like his visits to Miranda on the third floor are a big secret anyway. Everyone knows about him and *his girl*."

My tongue stuck to the roof of my mouth. I had to

pry the appendage off to get it to function. "Third floor you said?" My voice quaked.

She tapped away on her keyboard. "That's right."

"Thank you." I turned around, my body going through the motions of moving without any help from my brain. When I made it to a chair in a vestibule, I sank into the cushion, my knees giving out.

Drew and another woman? Someone named Miranda who everyone knew was "his girl"? The words were English and lined up as complete sentences, and yet they didn't compute. They didn't make sense at all. Finding Greg cheating on me had been a shock, but somehow also not surprising. If that made any sense. But Drew? I just couldn't see it. No matter how immature or flippant I'd once thought him, I'd never pictured him as someone who'd cheat. That definitely hadn't changed after all the time he'd spent pursuing me in his own goofy way.

Did I not know him as well as I thought I did?

That didn't seem possible either. So what was the truth? What everyone at the hospital seemed to consider common knowledge—Drew and some woman named Miranda—or the Drew that I knew and, if the bruising of my ribs by the beating of my heart was any indication, possibly loved?

Most women in my position would probably run away. Maybe go home, have a good cry, and down a few pints of Ben and Jerry's. They'd screen their calls and refuse to talk to the man who'd done them wrong.

After all, this scenario had played itself out in my life before. Maybe I was just the type of woman that men cheated on.

It would have been easy to give myself over to those types of thoughts, but what good would that do?

My fingers curled around the chair's armrests, and I pushed myself to my feet.

I'd come to the hospital to talk to Drew, and I'd be hanged if I left before I did just that.

Although, the noose would slip around his neck if I found him and another woman in the supply closet I'd imagined earlier.

There'd really only been two outcomes possible between me and Drew from the day we'd met. I'd either murder him in a fit of rage and annoyance, or I'd fall madly in love with him.

Please let it be the second one.

There was still the chance that my instincts weren't completely unreliable. That Drew hadn't just been playing one of his many games with me. That he was as serious as he'd claimed regarding us.

When I stepped off the elevator onto the third floor, soft strains of violin music welcomed me. Not from a recording or stereo either. Someone was playing an instrument in the hospital. But who? And why?

The soles of my shoes padded softly down the corridor, the music getting louder with each step. The hall opened to an atrium, and there, in the center of the room, stood Drew, his wooden instrument tucked snug between his chin and shoulder.

A pale child sat in a wheelchair in front of him, tubes connected to an IV hanging at her side. There were other kids scattered around the room listening to the music, but Drew seemed to be playing mainly for the girl.

A girl I'd bet was named Miranda.

Drew pulled the bow along the strings of the violin, but still I felt the motion deep in my chest, as if heartstrings were real and he was playing mine.

Emotion clogged my throat as tears sprang to my eyes.

As if he could feel my presence, Drew looked straight at me. His face appeared the same as it always did—square jaw, Roman nose, and a soft cleft in his chin barely visible. Yet his eyes were changed, though they held his unique shade of ginger, the lightest brown I'd ever seen. They contained a heaviness I'd never witnessed before in his gaze. There was no court jester joking in his orbs. No dancing or merriment in his irises.

He looked back to the girl and made the violin sing a serenade. A tear rose over my bottom lid and slid down my cheek.

I'd been right. Drew Bauer wasn't the cheating kind. He was the visiting the sick kind. And brightening someone else's day kind. Helping single mothers kind.

And—I swallowed past the lump in my throat—the easy to love kind.

His bow slowed, the last note humming through the air. With a sad smile, he lowered his instrument. A smattering of applause followed. He rested his gaze back on me.

I'm sorry, I mouthed. For taking away his voice after the confrontation with Greg, but also for doubting him, even for a moment.

A touch of familiar brightness returned to his countenance, and he held out his hand to me. It seemed symbolic, his invitation. Hadn't that been what he'd been doing all along? Inviting me to let go? To laugh? To live again? To love again?

I stepped forward and put my hand in his. Hoped he saw the gesture for all that it was.

"Two of the most important women in my life meet for the very first time." He gently pressed my fingers. "Nicole, I'd like you to meet Miranda."

I let go of Drew so I could properly greet this young lady who so obviously meant a great deal to Drew. "It's nice to meet you."

Her hand was limp in mine. "You too," she wheezed.

My heart clenched. The poor lamb. My eyes pricked as Drew's warm palm came to rest at the small of my back in support.

"You two have a lot in common." An almost imperceptible quake entered Drew's baritone. "You're both fighters."

A woman about my own age approached and gripped the wheelchair's handles. "And fighters need their rest for battle."

"Bye, Drew." Miranda waved.

Drew and I watched until Miranda had been pushed out of sight.

He picked up his violin case. "How did you know where to find me?"

"A receptionist informed me of your location and that you were with 'your girl.'"

He stopped me with a hand to my elbow. "You must have thought…" He shook his head. "I'm sorry I put you through that, even for a minute."

"Relax. You didn't."

"So you didn't storm down here wanting to tear into my hide?"

Visions of supply closets popped into my head. I pressed my lips between my teeth. "Let's just say I'm glad my intuition didn't fail me."

He searched my eyes. "Thank you."

"For what?"

"For not jumping to conclusions."

I leaned forward and pressed a kiss to his lips.

His smile quirked. "What was that for?"

My grin turned saucy. "For not making me exterminate you."

He threw back his head and laughed.

22

DREW

"How's this?" I came to a stop, grains of sand shifting and finding their way over the edge of my sandals and between my toes.

Ginny held an arm around the bundle strapped to her chest in an endless length of fabric she'd wrapped and tied around herself, securing baby Isaac to her person. She lifted her other hand to her brow to block out the glare of the sun. Swept her gaze up one side of the beach, then the other.

Waves swelled farther out from shore, surfers in wetsuits either bobbing with the flow or lying on their boards, arms diving into the water to catch the crest, push up to stand, then ride the wave for as long as they could.

My sister had better think the spot decent. The wagon filled with beach chairs, pop-up shade, sand toys, towels, and snacks wasn't exactly the easiest to pull across the loose sand. Plus, I'd told Nicole we'd be near lifeguard station number three. If Ginny dragged us any farther away, then I'd be made a liar.

"Here's good," she finally said.

I let the wagon handle go and went about unpacking the beach tent. Between Eric and me, we had the thing pitched with chairs set up beneath its shade in no time.

Owen took a soda from the cooler and popped the lid close to my face, the fizzy sound almost drowning out the waves for a second. I looked up at him from my seated position. He smirked at me. Annoying brat. My job as an uncle was done. I made like I was going to sprint after him with some sort of punishment when really, I had no intention of exerting so much energy. As predicted, he fell for my fake and raced across the beach.

"Too bad Mom couldn't be here." Ginny dug into the little kangaroo pouch she'd created and lifted the baby out, settling him in her arms.

I drummed my fingers against my knee. "Not like you aren't going to report back to her, I'm sure."

She didn't even try to deny the accusation, just lifted a shoulder to her ear. "Nicole's the first woman you've shown any serious interest in since Veronica. I'm sure dating's changed since Eric asked me to be his girlfriend in high school, but I'm also pretty sure introducing a woman to your family is still a big deal."

"I like her," I admitted. Why downplay my rapidly growing feelings? "A lot."

Ginny kissed her son's downy head. "Good."

My phone vibrated in my pocket. I fished it out, anticipation thrumming through my veins.

Eric laughed. "You've got it bad, man. Only a woman can make a guy's face go all soft like that."

I stood. "You'd know. Your mug's been goofy since the day I met you—which just so happens to be the day you met my sister."

Ginny reached over and smooshed Eric's face, pouting her lips as she said, "I think his mug's adorable." She moved his jaw back and forth.

Looked more like a fish face the way she squeezed.

"Thanks, honey," he said through mashed lips. He turned his face and kissed her. Without taking his eyes off Ginny, he waved me away. "I've got my girl. Go get yours."

I nearly ran into Owen as I stumbled over a tent peg. "I wouldn't go in there if I were you."

He looked past me, his brows dipping in disgust. "Are they kissing again? Gross."

I swallowed down a chuckle. One day he'd realize how *not* gross kissing was, but hopefully not anytime soon. "Want to come with me and give them some privacy?"

He fell into step at my side. "Sure. Where are you going?"

"Sierra and her mom just got here."

"Cool."

Two figures—one taller than the other—walked from the parking lot.

"I see them." Owen took off at a jog.

A more mature man would continue walking at a sedate pace. Hide his eagerness. Maintain decorum.

I grinned, then pushed the ball of my foot into the sand to catch up with Owen.

Good thing I'd never claimed to be a mature man.

Nicole was laughing by the time I reached her. "You'll never grow up, will you?"

I stopped in front of her and grinned. "Do you want me to?"

Her hair swung from side to side as she shook her head. "Absolutely not, Peter Pan."

I slipped my arm around her waist and pulled her to me, her hand resting on my chest. I hoped she felt the beat of my heart, the evidence of what she did to me. "I'm old enough to do this." I lowered my mouth to hers and pressed a kiss to her lips.

"Ew, Uncle Drew." Disapproval coated Owen's voice. "Let's go, Sierra."

Nicole chuckled, her mirth vibrating against my mouth. My smile grew above her lips, severing the contact. "We sure know how to clear a crowd." I threaded my fingers with hers.

"But we might need to brush up on our flirting." Laughter made her words come out like a song. "I think our exchange there might have skirted a line."

I replayed our dialogue, cringing as I heard what she referenced for the first time. "Not my intention."

"Nor mine." She leaned into my shoulder. "Maybe we just need more practice?"

My brows jumped to my hairline. My serious, strait-laced, no-time-for-games Nicole wanted to play. Something wild in me broke free, and I growled. "I like the way you think."

I let go of her hand, meaning to make a grab for her, but she anticipated my plans and side-stepped my swipe.

She laughed, and I growled again, stalking her as a predator would its prey. Nicole had always been beautiful in my eyes, even when she'd tried to be Atlas, taking the world on her shoulders. But now, as her eyes danced and her laughter floated on the ocean's currents and she spun away from my outstretched arm, she was radiant. The most bewitching woman I'd ever met.

And she'd put me under her spell.

Her foot slipped in the sand. I darted forward, snaking my arm around her waist and lifting her off her feet, her back to my front. Her head fell back and rested on my shoulder.

"Caught ya." I grinned into her eyes.

She stared back into mine. "That's because I quit running."

I set her back on her feet but didn't loosen my grip on her hips. I wasn't ready to let her go. Settling my chin on her crown, I peered out into the Pacific. "I'm glad it's still warm enough to come out here and enjoy the ocean."

"And I'm glad it's cold enough that no one expects me to wear a bathing suit."

My fingers reflexively curled into the soft swell covering her hip bone. "That's a sight I'd like to see."

The corners of her lips twisted into her cheeks, her expression dismissive. "Trust me, no one wants to see that."

I pulled her back and wrapped my arm around her, anchoring her to me. "I'm trying to think of how I can word this to convince you how wrong you are without sounding like I'm objectifying you in any way," I whispered into her ear.

She shivered in my arms. Not from the temperature. It wasn't that cold.

"Even before Sierra, I never had what people consider a beach body. And pregnancy and motherhood take a physical toll on a woman's form. Places that might have been firm once now sag. Not to mention stretch marks that look like crevasses on the surface of a glacier."

My little green queen. Only she would make such a comparison. I tilted my chin and pressed a kiss to the curve of her neck. "Beauty comes in all shapes, sizes, forms, and colors. God didn't have a mold when He created the world, and we don't need to try to put people into molds now." My hand slid across her stomach. "And the changes your body underwent to bring a life into this world are nothing to be ashamed of or hide. They're evidences of a miracle, sacrifice, and unconditional love."

Her palm covered the back of my hand. For a minute I thought she'd remove my hold, uncomfortable with me touching an area of her body she felt was less than beautiful. But instead of pushing my hand away, she pinned my palm to her navel.

Gratitude washed over me like the surge of the tide climbing up the coastline. Instead of shutting me out, she was letting me in. To the vulnerable places. The unguarded tender shoots of her heart.

I splayed my fingers, our position not lost on me. Expectant parents often stood like this, a soon-to-be father physically protecting his unborn child with the length of his hand. But Nicole wasn't pregnant, and I'd never feel my flesh and blood move under my palm in the womb.

I waited for the kick of loss, but instead felt only a twinge. Maybe that would never go away, but it no longer overshadowed the hope of other options.

"Would you ever consider more kids? Adoption or fostering?"

Her shoulder blades pressed into my ribs, reminding me to breathe.

"I'd always wanted to adopt. Never really had the burning desire to experience pregnancy myself, but Greg wanted his own progeny. Of course, I'd never trade Sierra for anything now though." She turned her head, her face in profile. "That dream hasn't changed, even if my life has."

I hugged her tighter. "You're an incredible woman." One I didn't want to share at the moment, though my sister and her family waited. I released my hold and offered my hand instead. "Come on, before my sister sends her husband out here to drag us back."

Her fingers settled against mine. We picked our way through the soft sand until the ground firmed from the beating of the waves. Ginny stood outside the shade shelter, Isaac in her arms. She beamed at us as we neared.

"I apologize in advance for anything my sister may say," I muttered in a volume loud enough for Nicole but not so loud as to get me in trouble.

"You've met my mother. If we made crazy family a contest, I'm sure I'd win."

Hands down. Shirley was in a league of her own.

"I'm so glad to finally meet you, Nicole!" Ginny hugged her with one arm, twisting so as not to squish the baby.

Nicole patted her back. "You too." She nodded to Eric. "Coach Eric."

He dipped his chin. "How are you, Nicole?"

"Good. Thanks." She stepped back and peered at Isaac swaddled in his blue blanket with cartoon whales. "And who's this handsome man?"

Ginny brought him forward with pride. "This is our little Isaac."

Nicole bent over, crooning baby noises.

"Do you want to hold him?" Ginny asked.

Nicole's eyes lit. "May I?"

"Of course." Ginny passed the bundle. Nicole cradled him in the crook of her elbow, swaying gently back and forth. She started humming a soft and slow tune.

Our previous conversation of adoption couldn't have been more disastrously timed. Now all I could see was Nicole with *our* baby in her arms.

I was getting ahead of myself. Again.

And yet...

"What's that tune you're humming?" Ginny asked.

Nicole lifted her head from staring into baby Isaac's face. "Oh. His blanket reminded me of this little lullaby my mom used to sing to my brother of a whale swimming in the sea and all the adventures he got into."

"Your brother the marine biologist?"

Her mouth twisted in humor. "That's the one. Mom sang her will over him, and now he's literally devoted his life to saving the whales."

Ginny laughed. "Is that how it works? Maybe I need to call Owen back here and speak words of industry over him. That boy is lazier than a sloth on Prozac."

"Leave the kid alone," Eric said.

Sierra and Owen had discarded their shoes and rolled their pant legs up. They were busy chasing the receding water on the shore, then racing the following surge.

"He doesn't seem so lazy now," I pointed out, knowing the contradiction would irk her.

Sure enough, she folded her arms.

"He ran pretty quickly to try and block for Sierra at the game, too," Nicole said before Ginny could call me out. "I appreciated his hustle."

Ginny puffed out her cheeks. "I can see when I'm beat. Also, nice teaming up there, you two."

"We do make a nice team, don't we?" Nicole shot me a lopsided smile, admitting to taking my side in that verbal spat, if it could be called that.

"How so?" Ginny would get her digs in somewhere.

"We are opposites in a lot of ways," Nicole conceded. "And at first, that's all I could see."

"And now?" I asked. Guess Ginny wasn't the only one digging. I knew Nicole returned my feelings, but I wanted to hear it. Call me greedy.

"Now I can see how our opposites are strengths and not a weakness. I never needed anyone to complete me, because I'm a whole person on my own. But I didn't know I needed someone to complement me, and you do that. We do that—together. You make me a better person. A more rounded person. You see my passion for what it is, not drama, and instead of wanting to quiet me, you encourage my zeal, even to the point of fighting alongside me." Her smile turned secretive, and I knew we were both thinking of Joshua Trees. "You still drive me crazy, but I've decided to see that trait as charming rather than annoying."

My heart swelled. She'd said everything I'd thought so perfectly.

"You must have it bad, then, if you think Drew's charming instead of annoying." Ginny groaned.

I shook my head. Nothing like family to ruin a moment.

23

NICOLE

*M*ost people rocked out to old classics on road trips, or if they had kids, the latest popular animated movie sound track. Not Sierra and me. We cruised up Interstate Five blaring NPR on the AM radio. The hot topic of discussion was a peace treaty being brokered between the leaders of multiple Middle East nations.

"Are we there yet?" Sierra asked from the backseat.

Okay, so my daughter was wise beyond her years, but she was also still only eight.

My index finger pushed up on the blinker, and I tilted the steering wheel slightly to get onto our exit. "About twenty more minutes."

"How big do you think Snoopy has gotten?"

Last time we'd been at Malachi's ranch, a new baby calf had just been born. Much to the quiet rancher's consternation, and Jocelyn's encouragement, Sierra had named the doe-eyed newborn. Snoopy, for the time he played the Red Baron and after the bovine's reddish-brown coat.

"I'm not much of a cow expert, but you could ask Mr. Malachi. He probably knows."

I watched in the rearview mirror as she pressed her nose against the window. "I don't want to remind him how many pounds of ground chuck Snoopy will yield."

"Oh, sweetie pie."

The crossbeams of the Double B brand stood erect over the driveway. I pulled my car under their shadow, wincing when the front right tire sank into a crater of a pothole with a jerk. As much as I loved my electric car, it didn't tackle country roads quite as well as Drew's gas-guzzling SUV. Pebbles crunched in the tires as I inched forward, slamming into another divot.

After I was sure I'd be forking out a month's wages to a mechanic to replace my car's suspension, we made it to the end of the drive and parked in a clearing.

"Finally," Sierra breathed. I silently echoed her sentiment.

I popped open the door and stepped out, stretching my legs. My nose wrinkled immediately. Jocelyn had been right to fall in love with the landscape of this place—and its reticent owner—but I wasn't sure how she'd get used to the distinct smell. Each cow could produce thirty to fifty gallons of greenhouse gases a day. Not sure how big Malachi's herd was, but even these wide-open spaces couldn't dissipate all those cow farts and burps.

The screen door slapped against its wooden frame as Molly pounded down the porch stairs. She flung her arms around my neck in her exuberant way, squeezing with the strength of a boa constrictor.

"If you don't loosen your grip, you're going to be down one bridesmaid."

Her arms fell away, but as she stepped back, she looked far from chagrined. "I'm just so excited. I'm getting married!"

Betsy appeared at her side. "We know," she drolled. "And now Nicole is finally here, we all get to practice walking slowly in a straight line and standing still. Rehearse things we've all mastered since we were toddlers. Super good use of our time."

"Sorry we're late. Traffic through Los Angeles was awful."

Molly waved away my apology. "We weren't ready to start until now anyway." She led us behind the house.

White folding chairs had been set up with a wide aisle running down the middle for the wedding party and then the bride to walk down. At the end of the aisle stood a garden arbor in its natural wood tone. Sunflowers, gerbera daisies, grevillea, poms, and other flowers had been arranged in a beautiful assortment and attached to the corner to cascade down the wooden beam's side. On the ground stood overflowing pots of orange, yellow, and purple chrysanthemum.

"This is beautiful, Mol." I managed past my tightened throat.

She squeezed my arm and whispered, "I'm getting married."

The first of our group to do so. (I wasn't counting my marriage to Greg in this equation.) But probably not the last...

Off to the side, speaking in low tones together, Malachi and Jocelyn caught my eye. Malachi looked down at her with the same adoration Ben gave Molly.

"They should make it a double wedding and be done with it." Betsy rolled her eyes.

Molly's eyes rounded. "That's the best idea ever."

I tightened my grip on her arm. "Don't rush them. And let's focus on one bride for today, hmm?"

"Are we ready?" Molly and Ben's pastor had taken a stand in front of the arbor.

My neck turned, and I scanned the area. Where was Drew? A few rows up front were occupied, but not by Drew. They didn't hold a head of hair I'd been dreaming of running my fingers through for days now. No, from the looks of it, those were Molly's and Ben's parents.

I kept turning, waiting to be held in his ginger gaze. This was who I'd become. That woman who searched a room for her man. Waiting for the connection that could span the distance. Not that I needed him for strength, although he made me stronger. Or for comfort, although he eased my worries. No. I looked for him simply because I wanted to be with him.

Laughter boomed from behind me. I craned my neck even more, a pinch forming in my shoulder. Our gazes collided. The lines around his eyes softened. One lid lowered as the corner of his lip tilted up in a flirtatious wink. He clapped Ben on the back and sauntered toward me with a huge grin on his face.

I swallowed down my corresponding smile as Betsy and Molly walked away from me to congregate with the others by the pastor. Betsy had been right though. How much practice did one need to walk and stand still?

Drew's grin turned a bit wolfish as he approached. A thrill shot down my spine. I'd always thought playing games was a waste of time.

I'd never been more wrong.

"Don't you know weddings are a serious event?" I scowled up at Drew, using all my control to appear annoyed when I really wanted to laugh.

Drew's cheek twitched. He knew what I was doing. Issuing a challenge. Wanting to play. "Oh yeah? And here I thought they were a happy occasion filled with joy."

"Am I going to have to separate you two?" Molly asked with a teasing glint in her eye.

Drew captured my hand. "I'd like to see you try."

But he let me go after kissing my knuckles and took his place as best man next to Ben.

Molly led her entourage of bridesmaids to the beginning of the aisle, and we all practiced our slow walk to the front. I held my invisible bouquet out in front of me and took the first step forward. When a baritone voice starting singing, I faltered—both my step and my lips. I looked up and met Drew's gaze. He added volume to his voice as he sang the lyrics to *Make you Feel My Love.* His exaggerated twang made the muscles in my face bunch.

Must. Not. Smile.

I continued my slow march, my eyes never leaving his. By the time I stood off to the side of the pastor, my cheeks hurt. I quirked a brow at him, silently asking, *Is that all you've got?*

"Is that part of the ceremony?" The pastor inquired, clearly confused.

Ben glared at Drew.

Drew held up a hand then pointed to me. "She started it."

Ben assessed me. I kept my face neutral. Ben really only knew me as the zealous environmentalist. When given a choice between me or Drew starting shenanigans, Drew would be the clear culprit.

Obviously, Ben thought so as well. "Don't blame Nicole. Now, be serious so we can get through this."

Amanda walked down the aisle next. Drew stared at

me. I stared back. Neither one of us paid attention to the mock ceremony.

You got me in trouble, he mouthed.

I shrugged my shoulder, feigning innocence.

His eyes surged, and I felt the warmth all the way down to my toes.

"Then I pronounce you husband and wife," the pastor declared. "Should we go through it one more time?"

A collective groan echoed a cow's moo.

"I think they've got it." Ben's mom stood from the front row. She clapped her hands. "Now we eat. I've prepared a Greek feast for you all."

The wedding party filed out. Amanda stepped to my side. "Do you think if I gave her a Bundt cake, she'd put a potted plant in the center?"

"Amanda," I scolded.

"Or maybe she has a bottle of Windex in her purse in case one of us gets a scrape."

I sliced a glower at her. "I really can't believe the words coming out of your mouth right now."

She laughed. "I'm only teasing. Although I wonder if there's any truth to it, since Nia Vardalos is Greek after all."

"How about you just eat the Moussaka and don't say anything else outrageous."

Her eyes sparkled. "Saying outrageous things is your bit. Although maybe you're too preoccupied with a certain doctor to make statements about the decline of our planet?"

I watched Drew as he chased Sierra and Ben's daughter, Chloe, in a game of tag. "Not preoccupied, but maybe my sharp edges are finally being rounded out."

The wedding ceremony went without a hitch. The day dawned all blue skies and fluffy white clouds. There weren't any last-minute disasters of rips in hems or the cake not showing up. No one tripped down the aisle or fainted from having their knees locked and standing too long. The whole thing had been picture-perfect, and now Molly was Mrs. Reed... or she would be after a long wait at the social security office.

Malachi and his family had transformed one of their barns into a reception hall. Twinkly lights swagged from the rafters, and white linens had been draped on round tables. Mums and sunflowers added color. Rustic charm at its finest.

But the best part was the overwhelming joy on both Molly's and Ben's faces. As well as little Chloe. I didn't think I'd seen any of them stop smiling all day.

I hadn't stopped smiling either. Yes, because I was happy for my friends, but also for other reasons. Okay, one reason: Drew. The little looks he gave me that made me feel seen and special. The small touches that had awareness tingling up and down my arms.

And for all the attention he paid me, he showered as much on Sierra. I dabbed at the corner of my eye, liquid emotion spilling over. Drew had marched over to my little girl and bowed over an extended hand like a prince would to a princess, asking her to dance. She'd blushed and taken his hand, and he'd led her to the dance floor. Now they swayed to the music, Sierra standing on the top of Drew's feet as he taught her the steps of the dance.

Maybe it was the wedding or watching the two of them, but I found my thoughts on a certain path. That of the future. I no longer asked myself if I could imagine a future *with* Drew. Now I asked if I could imagine one *without* him.

The answer was a resounding no.

The music stopped, and Drew bowed again, gallant as any lord to his lady. Sierra giggled and dropped to a curtsy.

"Come on girls. Time to throw the bouquet." Molly grabbed her flowers and skipped to the edge of the cleared dance floor.

A presence filled the space behind me. Drew's arms came around my waist, his cheek to my temple. "You snatch those flowers out of the air like Lynn Swann in Superbowl Ten."

My chest rumbled. "I have no idea who that is."

He growled. "Just catch the bouquet, woman."

I turned in his arms to face him. "You do know what catching the bouquet means, don't you?"

He leaned his forehead on mine and stared into my eyes. "I don't care if anyone else thinks it's too early to say it. I've been saying things to you prematurely from the beginning. Why stop now? I love you, Nicole."

He loved me.

Some women would have melted from such a declaration. Me? My spine turned to iron. I pressed up on my toes and kissed him hard on the mouth. "Those flowers are mine, Bauer."

His chuckle followed me as I made my way to the crowd of women.

To my right, Malachi stood in front of Jocelyn, his hands on her shoulders, his gaze intent on her face. She seemed determined as she dipped her chin. Malachi removed his Stetson and set it on top of Jocelyn's curls, the headwear looking as much a part of her as her flowing gown did.

"I love you, but don't get in my way," she warned as she took the spot beside me.

I bent at the knee and did a little boxing dance, shaking my hands out at my sides. "Back at ya."

Molly stood in front of us. "Ready?" She turned around to face the other way.

I crouched, poised. Jocelyn bumped me with her shoulder.

The bouquet sailed up in the air. Up and over our heads.

No!

I watched as it arched down toward Betsy. Betsy's eyes widened, and she batted at the air, eventually hitting the flowers, which bounced and landed...

In Amanda's hands.

Amanda blinked, then laughed nervously. "Good thing I don't believe in this kind of stuff."

I'd half a mind to tackle her for those flowers. I dug my toe into the ground.

Malachi pulled a slump-shouldered Jocelyn from the fray. Then I felt Drew's fingers encircle my wrist. He tugged until I stood in front of him, and he set my palm on his chest over his heart.

"They're just flowers." His words rumbled in my ear.

They were *not* just flowers.

He cupped my jaw. "I'll marry you even if you didn't catch the silly bouquet."

Time stilled. Was he...

"I'm not proposing. Not now. Even I know that may be rushing things a little too much." He tilted my chin up, his eyes intense. "But one day." His thumb caressed the apple of my cheek, a hint of a smile playing at his lips. "I'm happy to know that when I do ask, you'll say yes."

A tell-tale twinkle entered his eyes. The same that always came when he tried to goad me or said something he knew would get a reaction from me.

I pulled back just a touch. I didn't really want to

leave the circle of his arms. "I never said that."

"You were about to rip that bouquet out of Amanda's hands."

I shrugged. "They are really pretty flowers." They weren't *that* pretty.

His fingers pressed into my lower back. "Nothing to do with me or the fact I told you that I love you?"

A zing went through my heart. I didn't think I'd ever get tired of hearing that.

His head dipped, and he nuzzled my neck. "I used to imagine kissing you speechless. Never thought I'd have to use the same technique to get you to talk."

My lips curled but remained seamed together, daring him to do just that.

His mouth found the underside of my jaw. Skimmed across my cheek. His nose made a circle around the tip of mine.

My lips parted, every part of me focused on that patch of skin, willing him to kiss me properly already. His mouth hovered over mine. I reached up and cupped the back of his head. He was toying with me, but I was done playing this game.

I pulled his face down to me. His eyes flashed with victory. Silly man. He may have thought he'd won, but I was the one claiming my prize.

My lids lowered and mouth softened as I met his lips. A kiss could say a thousand things, but I put only one message into mine. Then, in case he missed it, I pulled back and murmured, "I love you, too, Drew."